Blood Empire

Blood Empire

A Time of Fear & Flight

SYDNEY KNOX

Followed by:
Blood Empire
Book Three:
A Day for Tears & Triumph

Dedication:

For the men who have made a difference in my life –
my grandfather Warren B. Stewart, my father William
Bigger, and Maurice Hunt. Each taught me
something, loved me unconditionally and changed my
life for the better.

Table of Contents

Major Players & Important Details

Flavius Crispus

Son of Constantine
Currently on the run from his
father, ambitious hothead
with a good heart, accused
of a terrible crime

Constantine

Western Augustus of Rome,
At work on a plan to take
control of the Roman world,
has a weakness for his
wife and his Christian mother,
military genius, bad father

Fausta

Empress of Western Rome
Daughter of the former
Augustus Maximian and
Constantine's troublemaking
wife, loves her children
to a fault, a woman on a
mission with bad intentions

Maxentius

Western Augustus (Usurper)
Son of the former Augustus
Maximian, and brother of
Fausta, Heavy drinker with
more luck than talent, smart
enough to let his betters do his
work for him

Maximian	*Former Western Augustus of Rome* Friend to the founder of the Tetrarchy, Diocletian, ruthless schemer who clawed his way to the top and taught his children to do the same, failed usurper and dirty old man
Licinius II	*Son of Licinius I (Western Augustus of Rome)* First cousin to Crispus and his best friend, skilled warrior and unapologetic joker, loves wine and women in that order)
Julia	*Daughter of Galerius (Eastern Augustus of Rome)* Childhood friend of Crispus & Licinius, hopeless tomboy, fearless and a smart fighter, stubborn and impatient with fools and whiners
Messalina	*Fausta's body slave* Beautiful and sensuous slave who will do anything and anybody for her mistress
Viatoro	*Crispus' Nisean Stallion* On the run too, through no fault of his own, too beautiful to hide away, loyal companion

Rome is divided into a Western and Eastern Empire. These divisions are meant to be ruled by a senior emperor, the Augustus and a junior emperor, the Caesar. It didn't work out quite that way; which often happens when bad ideas spring from good intentions.

Hierarchy of Roman Emperors in 310 AD:

Western Empire

- Licinius I is officially the Western Augustus but controls parts of the East instead. He is an ally of Constantine.
- Constantine is officially Caesar but considers himself the Augustus.
- Usurper Maxentius proclaims himself Augustus but controls only the city of Rome itself, the Italian peninsula and North Africa.
- Consequently, there is no junior emperor in the West.

Eastern Empire

- Galerius is the Augustus but is near death.
- Licinius I is the acting Eastern Augustus despite his official capacity as Western Augustus.
- Maximinus Daia is the Caesar but rises against Licinius in a bid to control the Eastern provinces.

When the sun rises in Rome the world wakes…

Far from home and with few friends left, Flavius Crispus is in a race for his life against his father, Constantine. Accused of a terrible crime, Crispus' panicked choice to flee Constantine's wrath places him forever at the mercy of strangers and new friends, a perilous condition at best. His troubles stem from one source, his stepmother Fausta whose designs for her future threaten to bring down the empire in a storm of blood and slaughter. Crispus' arrogance and pride become his downfall as Fausta uses his weaknesses against him in a plot to set him against his father and seize his birthright for her children.

His efforts to find his way to safety in the near East is aided by the appearance of his cousin Licinius and his childhood friend Julia Galeria, both children of Roman emperors, and both of whom end up with prices on their heads, courtesy of Crispus.

In the meantime, forces are at work to turn religious relics into weapons of war. The only thing standing between stability and chaos is Crispus and his grandmother Helena, who sends him on a quest to save her, himself and ultimately the father and nation that abandoned him.

When the world turns upside down, fear and flight can become noble pursuits for brave men seeking their place in it….

Chapter One:

House of Cassius

Italia - Early Winter, 310, Italia

"Why did I sleep with that woman?" It was a riddle with an impossible answer, one that men older and wiser than twenty-one years old Crispus surely asked themselves when chasing women led to trouble. It was bad business all around, and there was no easy fix. His father was Emperor Constantine, the Western Augustus of Rome, and he had placed a bounty on Crispus' head so high no sane man would refuse it.

Constantine had been fighting to secure his father Constantius Chlorus' dream of a Roman empire united under their house for five years, but final victory eluded him. Crispus had been chief among his father's men; he was a loyal son and an outstanding soldier. Yet, at that very moment, Crispus was fleeing into the night, his life threatened by the very person who gave it to him.

And it was all because of a woman. Not just any woman – the one woman in the world he should have kept at a distance but was too arrogant and truthfully too ignorant as well, to see the danger. Like most men he had to find out first hand that fire will indeed burn. Fausta, his father's wife was a temptress who lured Crispus to her bed and screamed rape when he refused her – or at least that was the story Crispus told Lactantius, his childhood tutor and friend. It was Lactantius who protected him when Praetorians came to arrest him in Laus Pompeia where he hid after fleeing Mediolanum in terror. And it was Lactantius who gave him a month's supply of food and sent him to Ariminum, to a Christian friend who could help Crispus escape his father's wrath. The friend, Marcus Cassius was a well-connected jeweler who could see Crispus safely to his Aunt Zenobia's home in Nicomedia, far away from Constantine's death sentence.

And now with his stallion Viatoro running at a breakneck pace, Crispus headed out of Laus and down the Via Aemilia with a heavy heart. After the frenzied confusion of his narrow escape from his father's Praetorians, he was left with only bitter disappointment to keep him company on the lonely road south. He rode for hours, his thoughts churning in endless circles. He finally stopped to rest and take a little wine (he resisted the temptation to drink the whole wineskin) and a few bites of the bread Lactantius had given him. When he fed a handful of rolled oats to Viatoro, the horse was so grateful, he felt ashamed. He knew he was pushing the stallion too hard, but there was little choice. The Via Aemilia was a road known for ambush, and it was risky to travel with a horse as fine as Viatoro, a prime target for any would-be bandits.

The Italian countryside stretched wide before him. A vast fertile region of low mountains with hazy green slopes stretched on forever into rolling plains planted with vineyards of ripening grapes and not far from them, marshy fields of rice. On the far side of the vast sweep of land were sand dunes where sea gulls flapped majestically between the sky and the blue-green waters of the Adriatic. The soft and warm underbelly of Italy was as hearty and varied as polus, the thick soup boiled in kitchens all over the land. Life in the countryside was bountiful, full of homespun flavor from the mix of Etruscan, Gallic and native Italians who lived amid the hills and overhanging rocks that stood watch over barren wheat fields plucked of one harvest and not yet pregnant with the next.

As Crispus neared Bononia, he shuddered involuntarily as he passed through the ruins of the Etruscan necropolis on the northern outskirts of the city. The marble monuments with their round stone adornments were several centuries old. It was a macabre coupling, the specter of death looming over his head and the reality of it spread out around him. He traveled through without slowing. The crumbling, moldy statues were the worst of it. They left him with dark thoughts in his mind, seeing the winged cherubs, fanciful beasts and tangled web of vines slowly engulfing them. It brought him too close to the feelings of despair that dogged and threatened him more than his father.

The eerie feeling remained with him as he sought out a comfortable, discreet stable where he could board Viatoro for the night. The stable master in the smallest, oldest stable in Bononia stared at the horse in awe as he and Crispus negotiated Viatoro's stay.

The bald and wrinkled little man stared at Viatoro as though he was Jupiter's own stallion.

"What a magnificent creature! Is he a Nisean? He sure looks like a Nisean." The stable master approached cautiously. He stroked Viatoro's mane and gave his head a pat. "I don't think I have ever seen a finer horse! Whoever you are stranger, you must be an important man to own him." The stable master was almost breathless with excitement. Crispus was quick to crush it. The less the stable master remembered of him the better.

"Nisean? I don't know about that but I do know that he is the kind of horse who has an owner who wants to be left alone and will kill curious stable masters who ask questions they should not. Understand me?"

The stable master nodded and hurriedly grabbed Viatoro's reins. He became very busy suddenly with stroking the stallion's massive head and whispering to him. Then he led him into the stables where clean water and fresh hay waited for him.

Satisfied the man was sufficiently cowed to submission and glad he did not have to haggle as though Viatoro were a melon in the market, Crispus settled on a dark little inn near the shore of the Reno River. Where it lacked cleanliness, it substituted cagey guests, the kind who ask no questions and give no answers.

Demanding privacy, Crispus had the innkeeper make ready an upper room, which Crispus suspected was actually a cupboard. Too exhausted to balk, he accepted it without complaint. He settled into the tiny space and lay down, but as tired as he was, sleep eluded him. He rose and looked out the window across the river while his mind raced down a winding path of self-torture. Crispus cursed his foolishness and abject failure again and again. He was needed in his father's army, not hiding in a rat hole in Bononia. *Damn that woman!* Anger and frustration boiled within him, and he was as restless as the black waters that flowed beneath the window. When sleep finally arrived, he greeted it as welcomed friend and immediately lost himself in it.

The following morning Crispus rose early. He immediately went to collect Viatoro from the stable master, who seemed sad to see him go.

"It is not often that I get to take care of an animal like this. I won't forget him!" The man's easy camaraderie evaporated when he saw Crispus' reaction to his praise.

Crispus moved close to the man, his hand near his gladius.[1] "I thought I told you last night, I see you need a reminder this morning. This horse was never here, and neither was I. If you value your life that is the story you will hold to."

Crispus felt a tinge of guilt for threatening the little man but he could take no chances. The frightened stable master nodded quickly, handed Crispus Viatoro's reigns and disappeared back inside, loudly bolting the door behind them.

Confident that no one in Bononia realized who spent the night among them, he headed for Ariminum. He had no idea what would be waiting for him there, friendly strangers or a bounty hunter's knife at his throat. He rode all day stopping only at nightfall when he could no longer navigate the darken forests he passed through on the way.

---

[1] Short, two-edged sword used by Roman soldiers.

By late the next morning though, he was crossing the Tiberius Bridge outside the city just as the sun reached the zenith of the day.

He headed directly to the forum. In worldly, seaside Ariminum, no one took notice of the pretty stallion and his hooded rider weaving amongst the crowded streets. They assumed he was just another high-born fop looking for entertainment in the city's dicier sections. There was safety in the assumption, no one cared a bit who did what to whom, or where they did it. Proving him right, the only people watching him were a leno and his prostitute who lost interest as soon as more appealing prospect approached them, a drunkard jangling a heavy purse.

The sex trade was thriving in the city and brothels were plentiful. Crispus passed several along his way, but resisted the temptation to ease his troubled mind in one of them. As much as he wanted to escape to the warm pleasures of a woman's body and the experience of leaving earth for heaven; it felt wrong. Coming so soon after his proclivities cost him everything, he felt ashamed that they should pull at him now, he simply did not have the stomach for it. Whether queens or whores, the games women played were all the same and he was too heartsick to suffer them, despite the obvious benefits.

Crispus moved on, passing through winding streets and in between the insulae that teemed with proletarii rushing about like so many little carpenter ants. It was a depressing sight. Downtrodden vendors stood in front of their makeshift storefronts. Limp thatched roofs hung soggy with undried morning dew, wobbly carts and weathered stands sagged, some even ready to buckle under the weight of produce, meat and dry goods piled high for demanding, haggle-prone customers.

Further down the way, toward the center of town, concrete buildings with covered doorways and columned porticos marked the better shops. They lined both sides of the cobbled streets near the Grand Basilica. Here things were different, the city was split into those with and without fortune in their lives.

Food and medicine shops, high end brothels and drinking holes sat beside one another, feeding off each other in an endless circle of excessive, reckless deeds subsequent regret, and a search for a remedy to fix it all. Dirty-faced children raced each other and chased the stray dogs that darted in front of the shops while the indignant owners shooed both back to the slums they came from.

Crispus stood taking in the bustling city around him. Too late, he realized to his dismay that he had no real idea of where Marcus Cassius lived. Lactantius had given him a general idea, but it proved useless now that he was in the city. Lactantius had obviously not been in Ariminum in some time, nothing Crispus saw thus far matched anything he told him.

Crispus decided to ignore the rabble around him. Most of those he passed would not know a luxury jeweler if he was squatting on a latrine next to them and said as much. He looked in vain for someone who at least appeared of sufficient means to be acquainted with a man such as Marcus Cassius.

At last, he spotted a tall, handsome youth who was close to his own age and fit the image he sought. The boy wore a nobleman's heavy tunic, made of fine wool, dyed a deep forest green, and with an extravagant cloak edged in gold and gathered with a jeweled brooch at his shoulder. A wizened old man shuffled along at his side. They looked like the kind of people who had too many of their own affairs to inquire too deeply into a stranger seeking help.

Crispus called out to him, making the assumption that the boy spoke the same refined and formal Greek that he did. "You there! Can you tell me where to find the domus of Marcus Felix Cassius?"

The boy looked at him strangely. Crispus began to wonder if Lactantius had given him the wrong name, or if the boy could not understand Greek after all. But a moment later, recognition dawned on his face and he suddenly brightened.

"Oh, you mean old Cassius, the goldsmith! Yes, I know him. I don't usually hear him called by his name. Around here, we call him Bubo. You're not far from him. You can follow me; I'll show you the way. My name is Titus Marcellinus, and this is Apollonius, my tutor."

Crispus and Titus set off together down the cramped, sloping streets. The aged tutor followed after them, with some difficulty at the fast pace. As they passed houses and shops, the buildings became larger and the houses more refined and elegant than those at the edge of town but were still rather plain. As in Rome, the finest homes seldom looked it from the outside, the better to hide from jealous thieves and cutthroats bent on plunder.

Crispus and his guide were silent as they walked, sharing the awkwardness of two strangers thrown together without warning. Titus's curiosity got the better of him finally, and he broke the silence with a question.

"If I may ask, are you a friend of Bubo's? He seldom sees people these days. My father was the last to visit him, and that was some time ago."

"I'm not. A mutual friend sent me to deliver a message." Thinking quickly Crispus seized on the name of a random soldier at his camp. "My name is Gallus Albus."

"Well in that case, Gallus Albus, I should warn you, I don't know that Bubo will allow you inside." Titus said. "There was a terrible affair a couple of years ago which cost Bubo his son's life. Since then the family has been in seclusion."

"Who lives with him?"

"Just his wife and daughter. He sold his business to his brother and swore he'd never touch another piece of gold."

Crispus was incredulous. "So he's a hermit then?"

"Well, I'll not say it, but others might. He took his son's death hard. They say some men angry about loss profits on a deal gone bad sent killers in the night. His guards managed to fight them off, but his son was killed in the fracas. He was only fifteen. It has been two years now and still, Bubo will not speak of it. He keeps the doors bolted shut to all except a trusted few and none but the slaves are ever seen leaving the house. It's quite the scandal, really."

"Faex[2]..." Crispus muttered in Latin and tried not to think about what would happen if Cassius should refuse him entrance. He had risked everything on Lactantius' word. At all costs, he could not be

---

[2] Curse word meaning feces

turned away, even if he had to bribe or threaten everyone in the household. "I will see Marcus Cassius or die trying." He muttered to himself but with such passion he knew he said it loudly enough for Titus to hear him.

The boy looked at him with a puzzled expression.

"Do you find me odd, Titus?" Crispus asked, realizing he probably appeared that way to the boy politely walking him to a hermit's abode.

Titus thought about it for a moment then shrugged. "No, not really. The same thing happens to me. I often get caught up in my thoughts too. It's a sure sign of cleverness if you ask me." He laughed then, long and hard – the way a boy laughs when he amuses himself if no one else.

Titus stopped walking and pointed a finger further up the street. "Bubo lives just over there, the one on the left. I would try going around to the servant's entrance if I were you. You'll stand a better chance of getting inside that way."

"Thank you, Titus. I'm glad to have met you. Perhaps our paths will cross again." Crispus offered a hand.

"I hope so. Ask for Aeneas, the household steward. If anyone can convince old Bubo to see you it's him," Titus said warmly, shaking his hand.

Crispus watched as Titus disappeared back into the crowds, his tutor huffing along behind him, trying to keep up. Then he turned towards the house with hesitation in his step. Crispus swallowed hard, then with all the confidence he could muster, he approached the house. After walking the perimeter a few times to check the lay of the things, he finally knocked at the back gate.

An eternity of waiting ensued. He began to think no one would answer at all but then a harassed, angry-faced woman appeared at the gate. She eyed him warily, as though his bedraggled appearance was a personal insult to her.

"What do you want?" She demanded. When he told her Aeneas, her frown increased.

"What do you want with Aeneas? My dominus does not like visitors and certainly not dirty, unannounced ones. Who are you?"

Crispus did not suffer her manner. She was slave after all, not the domina of the house. "I'm a friend of a friend, woman. Now, get Aeneas for me as I told you... now." He glared at her, daring her to refuse him, to deny the natural authority that wafted around him despite his appearance.

She looked him over slowly, sizing him up. Without another word, she spun on her heels and hurried away. She returned in short order with a bald, heavyset man Crispus assumed could only be Aeneas.

"Yes? What do you want here, stranger?" Aeneas asked, brows raised with the suspicion he reserved for all uninvited visitors who dared let their shadow fall on his master's door.

"I need to speak to your dominus. The teacher Lactantius sends me to him with an urgent message that I cannot deliver to except him."

At the mention of the beloved, well-known teacher Aeneas paused; his demeanor changed. "Lactantius? It has been many years since I heard that name. Is he well? He is a man greatly respected in this household. There is nothing amiss that brings you here, I hope." Aeneas lightly touched the small brass cross he wore on a thin, leather cord over his heart.

"He's quite well, thriving – and he sent me to Cassius. I have come a long way, and as I said, it is an urgent matter. You obviously share his faith; do you likewise respect his judgment on who can be trusted?"

Aeneas bristled as though Crispus offended him, but he remained calm. "Of course I do. Lactantius is a dear friend. Still, you must appreciate that my dominus does not see visitors since…" his voice trailed away at the mention of past horrors.

Crispus nodded. "I understand what happened here. I have heard the terrible story, and still I say to you, I must see your master. Now, will you allow me to see him or not?" Crispus stood his ground and looked the man in the eye. His intense gaze ended the stalemate between them and burned through the man's objections. Aeneas relented and stepped back to allow Crispus to enter.

"As you wish, sir. Follow me, please. And mind the floors of the culina. They're wet from scrubbing."

Aeneas led the Crispus through the kitchens where a pair of cooks were in the midst of preparing prandium[3] for the family. The old women stopped their slicing and grinding in curiosity. Crispus moved with a resolve and dignity that belied his appearance and the whispers about the handsome stranger began immediately.

A bubbling clay pot hung over the fire, and the delicious scent of stewed goose filled the entire kitchen. Crispus eyed the steaming pot, suddenly

---

[3] Small midday meal, similar to lunch

realizing he had not eaten since the previous day. He was famished, but he looked away when he noticed Aeneas watching him.

Aeneas laughed. "Smells good yes? Come back here before you leave and cook will give you a bowl of it to take with you."

It was Crispus' turn to be offended, "I'm no beggar, needing to carry scraps away. Aeneas. Just take me to your dominus," Crispus said sharply.

Aeneas raised an eyebrow at the rebuff to his misplaced kindness. Without another word, he led Crispus to a seat on a stone bench near the edge of the peristyle then left to fetch Marcus Cassius.

Resting against the cold stone, Crispus looked around him, taking in the unusual creation that was the house of Cassius. The peristyle had lavish appointments, with tall black marble columns and brightly painted statues in purples and deep reds. The path through the dense garden was the most unusual Crispus had ever seen, laid in alternating blocks of multi-colored marble and dark woods polished to a shine. A small stream of water ran between the statues, and heavy flora spilled into a small pool rimmed with a thick band of solid gold. It was beautiful in a garish way and no expense had been spared in its creation. Though the whole place reeked of a kind of wasteful vulgarity, Crispus understood how a man could barricade himself inside it and hide from the world.

When his host finally arrived at the edge of the garden, Crispus saw that the house was merely a reflection of its owner. Marcus Cassius was a large man and clothed in a finely-woven black tunic trimmed in gold thread. His hands, thick and round as pork sausages, were folded together before him and on each finger was a different jeweled ring. His neck was equally thick and his obvious love of gold culminated in several thick gold chains he wore around it. His brown hair was half-combed and wild, and his eyes betrayed sadness that was so stark it was uncomfortable to bear. His ostentatious displays did nothing to hide the deep mourning that marked him as much as his jewels marked his wealth.

Crispus stood to greet his host. "Salve, Marcus Cassius! Thank you for seeing me, I know you did not have to do so and I understand you are a private man. I will be brief," He added an optimistic "I hope you won't see my presence in your home as an imposition," but Cassius did not take the invitation to welcome him.

Instead, he regarded Crispus with a blank stare that looked through rather than at him. Moving slowly, he settled himself onto a nearby cushioned lounge while motioning Crispus to its twin, adjacent to him and away from the uncomfortable stone bench.

Cassius came right to the point. "Aeneas tells me you bring a message from Lactantius."

Crispus was blunt as well. "I am Flavius Crispus, son of His Excellency, Constantine Augustus. Lactantius is my friend – my last friend, unless you become one, which I hope you will. He sent me to you knowing you to be an honorable man, who would help the emperor's son."

He reached into his tunic and produced Lactantius' tiny sealed scroll. Cassius took it without a word. He examined the seal and the scroll itself for a long time before deciding it was genuine.

The seal broke with a snap. Reading the letter, Cassius tsk-tsked at Crispus, "Well, my boy you're in quite a bit of trouble, it seems." He added, "An emperor's wanted son comes to my house seeking aid. What am I to make of this messy situation dropped into my lap?" Shifting his girth more comfortably on the lounge, Cassius appraised his guest with a wary eye.

Crispus sat stone-still, although his stomach lurched painfully and his heart raced. He tried to hide his discomfort from his host. Coughing, he adjusted his tunic and ran an easy hand through his curls as though petitioning strangers, with his life hanging in the balance, was an everyday occurrence for him.

Cassius laid the scroll aside. When he spoke, the arrogance Crispus expected to hear had left his voice, replaced by compassion. "Well, Lactantius has never asked a favor of our friendship – you must be important to him to warrant one now. Lactantius knows I would never refuse under these circumstances."

Crispus spoke quietly. "He's like my father, sir. I trusted him by his word alone to come here and reveal myself to you, believing him that you would help me and not hand me over to my father to die." Crispus looked around him again. "Though I suppose you have no need for the emperor's reward. You have enough gold of your own."

Cassius shrugged. "That's true enough. I suppose there are men who would see this as an opportunity for advancement, but I do not. Lactantius sent you to me with a death order on your head, and I'll possibly bring one on mine for helping you. I can live with that. If I do this, it will be for the right reasons, not so that I can betray you for a reward later. I'll help you. Of course, it's my Christian duty. I'll do all I can, but you must be truthful with me. What is this trouble you're in? I trust Lactantius, but I want to hear from you that you will not place my family at risk."

Crispus was torn by the question. He had no other way to reach the safety of Nicomedia, but he hated to lie about something so important. He decided to take up a variation of the truth. "I fell headlong into a trap my stepmother laid for me. She accuses me of attacking her, something I did not and would not ever do. Your life nor your family's is not at risk. You have my word. My father is not an excessive man in his personal affairs. His wrath extends no further than me. Thank you for your help, and especially for your trust in me. It honors me, I shall never forget it."

Cassius let his finish. He was quiet for a moment, looking away into the distance, somewhere in his past or his future but his face carried a resolve that encouraged Crispus.

"The honor is mine. Lactantius is a dear and trusted friend. Yes, I can arrange safe passage for you to Nicomedia, but it will take time. You are welcome to stay as my guest until then. Aeneas will see to your comfort." Cassius motioned to Aeneas, who had been standing a discreet distance away. He raised himself from his chair with difficulty. With nothing further to discuss, he took his leave with a sad waddle that was painful to watch. His abject grief was plain even in how he moved. Crispus had seldom seen a man so broken by his circumstances.

The shame of leaning on a despondent man

whose hopes had fled him was a weight on the dignity of Crispus' heart. *This sorry state is my own fault,* he thought, *and a lesson I won't forget.*

Aeneas told Crispus to follow him and led him to the rear of the house, into a spacious room with a large sleeping couch. "Prandium will be served shortly. I recommend you visit the bath first – it's adjacent to the peristyle." He bowed to Crispus and left.

Alone and safe at last, Crispus lay down on the couch. Within minutes, he was asleep, only waking when Aeneas reappeared with fresh clothes, scented oils, and a more pointed request that he use the baths before joining his hosts for the afternoon meal.

Crispus sniffed at his underarms, conceding the point, his nose wrinkled at his own scent. He was more nervous about being turned away than he thought. "I suppose you're right. I don't want to offend my hosts at the first meal."

He was able to relax finally, enveloped in the warm embrace of Cassius' balnea. The bathing rooms were just as flagrantly extravagant as the rest of the house. Intricate gold inlaid frescos, mosaic tile and statues were everywhere. There was an overabundance of live flora of all kinds, the steaming waters were dyed a startling shade of blue and attended by quiet servants waiting with strigil and oil. A lute player strummed in the corner.

Crispus' belly rumbled, unpleasantly reminding him of his hunger. He could only assume the food in the house would be of similar standard to everything else. Cassius certainly enjoyed it, by his appearance. Crispus finished and dressed as quickly as possible. Then, he headed to the grand triclinium to meet his hosts.

Prandium is usually a light, festive meal, but in the house of Cassius, a fog of hard grief lingered on the perfumed air. His hosts were polite but their pain was beyond disguise. The domina, Caecilia was a plain-faced woman with thinning blonde hair that she wore in short ringlets which did not flatter her. She was trim and statuesque with a reserved bearing and very few adornments. She seemed an odd choice for a man like Cassius. Crispus had expected a bejeweled frump of a woman but instead Caecilia was sharp-featured and grim, even more so than her husband.

Neither said much during the meal; they left the entertaining to their daughter Cassia, who was a beauty Crispus could not help noticing. She had golden curls and bright green eyes of a shade he had never seen before. Her face was the only bit of brightness in a room full of dreariness.

Cassia blushed a bit as she spoke to Crispus. Her high-pitched voice cracked painfully with nervousness at times, but she was engaging and intelligent.

"Sappho is my favorite of the ancient poets. Her work amazes me. What do you think of her?" Cassia was only a few years older than Crispus in age, and shared his love of Greek philosophy, history, and art.

"Well, her ideas were unique for the time. She was the one who spent her days falling into and out of love with her disciples, wasn't she?' Crispus mused with a raised brow.

Cassia laughed then, in a sound as lovely and natural as water tinkling through a brook. The more

Cassia revealed about her interest, the more Crispus liked her. She was too pretty and too charming for him to ignore his reaction to her. He forgot Cassius and his wife were present and before he thought about what he was doing, he asked Cassia to give him a tour of the city the next day.

At this Cassius found his tongue at last. "A pleasant thought," he said firmly, "but Cassia will have to decline. Forgive us, but she does not leave the grounds without us. I can send Aeneas with you if you like."

Crispus had no choice but to accept, though he had no interest in a tour with the steward. He was encouraged to see that Cassia was frowning as well. The remainder of the meal passed uneventfully save Cassia's mischievous glances at Crispus when her parents were not watching her.

Cassius and his wife had lapsed into moody silence while Crispus and Cassia talked quietly to each other. If young Cassia's plan was to command his full attention, she succeeded. Crispus was enchanted by her and was sorry when the meal was over.

Later, when even the slaves were in bed, Crispus sat awake in his room, writing a letter to Julia by lamplight. It was the only thing he could think of to do with himself. Being with Cassia had excited him in an unexpected way. Yet, in the quiet of his room his thoughts turned to the girl who still commanded so high a place that another only served to make him pine for her even more.

He had endured a long day but rather than the restful sleep he hoped for, he had dreamed of Julia and their childhood in Nicomedia. The dream was so vivid, it woke him and he could find no peace until he had written to her. He was sealing the letter when a sharp rap at the door jolted him. He tucked the letter away inside a fold of his satchel and although he was wary of who might be knocking so late, he opened the door.

When Crispus saw Cassia was on the other side, his displeasure melted away. There was a pause while he wrestled with his conscience, but his lust won. Crispus stepped aside to allow her to come into his rooms. Cassia glanced once down the hall and rushed inside, her sheer stola sweeping the floor behind her.

For a space of time that was an eternity yet over in an instant, they stood face to face, hers upturned defiantly, daring him to send her away, his lowered in teasing acceptance of whatever cause had delivered her to him. Cassia began in a gush of emotion.

"It's wrong for me to be here I know, but I had to take the chance to see you alone." She touched his cheek, putting her body as close as possible to him, teasing him as though she knew well the arts of seduction.

She might have been altogether enticing, but for the whiff of desperation hidden behind her provocative manner. Crispus ignored it. Untapped nervous energy from being on constant guard, welled within him, as an arrow without a target. Turning down a willing woman was nearly impossible and he did not particularly care to try.

"You're right. I should send you away – your father has treated me well – but I see no harm in you staying." He went to the desk and pulled out the chair for her. "You took such a risk in coming to me; it would be foolish and cruel to deny myself the pleasure of your conversation."

"Abba keeps me here like a prisoner, it was worth the risk. I suppose you know that much. He means to protect my honor, but sometimes I feel as though I am the one who died, especially when living is all I want to do! But that's a story for another time and place. I came to you tonight because I want something from you, and I'll give you something in return." She stopped a moment. Crispus suspected she was summoning her courage for what was sure to be a tempting, if indecent proposition.

"May I, that is…" Cassia's already flushed cheeks went brighter still. She took a deep breath and came out with it at last. "Would you like to have me tonight, Crispus? I have never known a man like you. It will be our secret – I promise."

The last words flew from her lips so smoothly, he wondered how many times she had recited them to herself in her rooms, or to other men in this house.

"You are a beautiful fool, my dear," he said, touching her face with a mock compassion he learned to display during his years bedding army camp strumpets. "You don't know what you're saying. You're trying to give me something I don't yet deserve."

"But isn't that for me to decide? You are the emperor's son, his heir. I am a woman with passions, the same as you and I want to see if your strength and prowess extend beyond the battlefield. What could be more natural? Do you not want me as well?" She looked at him, a plea forming in her eyes, but before it could reach her lips where it would surely shame her, he made a feeble last attempt to dissuade her with the truth.

"Of course I want you, any man would and should – but I'm not one to go about casually taking a young girl's maidenhood in her father's house?" It was meant to flatter but a question to her all the same.

She laughed and understanding him, gave him his answer. "You assume too much Crispus. I did not say I have never been with a man. I said I have never known a man like you. There is a difference."

"So you coming to me is just a whim then, something to fill the boredom of your captivity?"

"If I said yes, would it change anything?"

Crispus tried to hide his surprise. "It might change a great deal. I'm not sure I like being used and if that's your game here…" He left unsaid what he would do, mostly because he had no idea. He was having trouble focusing on anything except the warm pleasures that might await him after her barely dressed invitation.

Cassia's continued to pour honey whispers from her lips, telling him, "I am not using you. You will enjoy it." She stopped to let the truth of that sink into him. "–And you need not fear my father. He sees nothing except his accounting books since my brother died, except to imprison me here. If my door were not so near the slave quarters I should go insane from boredom.

"What? You're bedding the serving boys? Cassia, do you really sink so low?

"Well, I won't say yes or no to that; but I will say this, I have no regrets. So the question is simple. Do we take our pleasure tonight or do we part ways wondering what might have been?"

Her boldness unnerved him; however, she had a point, and besides, he was in sore need of a woman's comforts. He seized her before either of them could think better of it. Crispus took her into his arms and crushed his mouth down on hers. He forgot about the letter he wrote to Julia, his heartfelt wishes for hers and his devotion to their friendship.

He forgot everything except the warmth of Cassia's thighs when she forced him to the couch and straddled him. When her fumbling hands found their target and guided him inside her, they moaned together. He clung to her, his lips perfectly fitting into the hollow of her throat while she arched her back, and his hands squeezed her backside. He lost himself in the moment, riding waves of passion that climaxed with her tongue deep in his ear, him deep in her body and Crispus allowed himself to drown and return to life. Cassia was well-pleased and as promised, so was he.

Early morning brought the sound of rooster's crowing from the stables into the house, waking Crispus from a restive sleep. He was grateful to find himself on his couch alone; Cassia had left without a word while he slept. The only proof of their night together was the heavy mix of exotic fragrances she wore, which mingled with their sweat and permeated his blankets.

He was overwhelmed with the sheer lunacy of his actions in the penetrating light of day. He had no guarantees Cassia was as discrete as she promised and it would only take one whisper in the wrong ear to bring matters to an unpleasant head. He slid slowly from his blankets and splashed cold water on his face. The icy chill invigorated him and brought back his

good sense. He was obviously not Cassia's first
seduction. Thus far, her father was entirely the fool
about her noctural wanderings, but it would not do to
provoke her into laying an accusation at his feet.

His disappointment in his own actions, the
shame-faced gloom that circled around him in a dark
fog, made him regret his behavior with all the guilt of
a petulant child. Crispus thought with pain about
Fausta's seduction and a cold seed of fear, distress
and distaste filled his belly. Women always had a
motive, capricious and vain though they may be, and
dealings with them always complex. After his mind
raced for an hour in indecision, he finally decided
what to do about his Cassia predicament.

Decisions made, he went out to join the
family for the morning meal. He found Cassia and her
parents in a small triclinium, eating thick slices of
olive-oil-soaked bread, baked fresh and giving off a
scent that made him realize how little he had eaten
the night before, and of course the meal included
plenty of mulsum[4], well-watered, given the hour.
Cassia all but ignored him, which he guessed was part
of her game, but Crispus looked away too, happy to
play it.

The remaining days with Marcus Cassius and
his family passed in a peculiar kind of emotional
whirlwind; everything felt slow except his mind,
which raced in circles leading nowhere. He avoided
Cassia at every opportunity. He maintained polite
interest at mealtimes of course but he ignored her late
night knocks on his door altogether, until she gave up

[4] Honeyed wine, popular in Rome

at last.

In place of Cassia, Crispus spent his time enjoying the city's various delights with his new friend Titus, forming a friendship bred of boredom and nurtured on expensive wines and cheap women. Titus admired Crispus for the natural sophistication and style he would never have living in tiny Ariminum. For his part, Crispus liked the free-spirited boy who lived a life with little stress and strife. They grew close and Crispus confided in Titus his true identity, though the two of them spun a tale of Crispus as a visiting relation from northern Italy when pressed at the better parties.

The pair of them cut fine figures as they prowled the city streets, reckless young gods set loose on the world. It was impossible for the simple folk of Ariminum not to notice their lecherous behavior in the public houses and brothels. If that bothered Crispus, he did not show it, but as the sailing date drew near, and his days cavorting with Titus grew tiresome, he found himself overcome with a strange melancholy he could not quite understand. It nibbled and gnawed at his stomach.

The pain worsened with the suspicion that somehow Julia was at the root of it. Despite his best efforts, no amount of wine he drank or poppy he smoked could rid him of it. Between Julia, Fausta, and now Cassia he was overwhelmed, and there was nothing he could do about it. *Women will be the death of me!* It was a thought he could not escape. Without fail, every action he took with a woman was the wrong one. How could he hope for better with Julia, if and when he make it to her?

And yet he hoped. Some small part of him

wanted to believe they could rekindle something between them. The letter he wrote to her lay hidden away, and he had changed it several times. He intended to give it to Cassius to send to Nicomedia ahead of him. From what had been several pages, he discarded most of his ramblings until it was only a few lines which said everything. There was no need to sign it. She would know it came from him.

> *Julia, you know me well. Do not believe what you may hear but give me a chance to explain. My friends are few, I hope I can count you among them.*

Julia was a bright spot of life for him, but she confused him too. Behind him lay the shame of what happened in Mediolanum with Fausta and in his future, the prospect of Julia's wrath in Nicomedia. He couldn't get far enough away from one to suit him, and did not know if he could survive the other. And all while he was running scared and hiding like a coward. When he added in necessity of having to dodge Cassia at every turn, he was almost ready to give up altogether…almost. When he thought he would go mad if something did not happen soon, Marcus Cassius woke him one morning with the news that his ship finally arrived, and he could sail that very night.

A few hours later Cassius and his family gathered together in the rear garden to see him off. Crispus kissed each one, wondering if Cassius noticed how Cassia moved to kiss him first and kissed his mouth rather than his cheek. If he did not, her mother did. She pulled her away with a frown at both

Crispus and her daughter.

Crispus' farewell to Cassius was the longest and most sincere. Crispus did not linger over gratitude knowing his guilt in having Cassia, even briefly made it ring false to his ears. "I cannot thank you enough for your kindness. You opened your home and risked your life for me. I will never forget it or fail to repay you one day."

Cassius favored him with a rare smile. "My dear boy, you have been most welcome. You have no debt with me. My reward is waiting for me beyond this life. I'm glad to know you enjoyed the hospitality of my house."

Cassia's sudden giggle brought another warning look from her mother.

Misunderstanding, Cassius continued. "We shall miss the excitement of your presence, if nothing else." He managed a laugh that surprised both his wife and daughter.

"Here. This is for you." He handed Crispus a sealed scroll. "When you reach Ephesus, go directly to the Library of Celsus. There is a hollowed out groove at the bottom of one of the columns. Place this scroll inside and return the following day at the sixth hour. Someone will meet you. I've arranged for my friends in Ephesus to provide you with lodging and safe passage from there to Nicomedia. And I'm sending your stallion to you overland in a caravan of horse traders. My friend Josephus is a merchant and admirer of stallions. Viatoro will be well cared for and no one will mark him as yours."

Crispus clasped the man's hands in his own. "Thank you, Marcus." He produced the note to Julia from inside his tunic. "If I could ask one more favor of your friendship, please see that this letter is sent ahead to Nicomedia, to the palace of Emperor Diocletian. It is for his granddaughter Julia, a very dear friend of mine."

Cassia blanched at the words, and rage flamed in her eyes before she could hide it. Understanding spread across Caecilia's face. She looked to Crispus, seeking the truth from him. Crispus blushed and could not meet her eye, so instead he ignored her altogether.

"Will you do this for me?" Crispus pretended he could not feel Cassia or her mother's eyes on his back. He knew Cassia felt humiliated and rightfully so, but he was leaving, and he did not expect he would ever see her again.

"Hmm? Yes, yes, of course. You have my word." Marcus Cassius was distracted at last by the interaction between his wife, daughter, and Crispus. He was confused by it, but he said nothing as he tucked the note into the folds of his garment. Crispus turned to leave. Over his shoulder, he heard Caecilia's voice following behind him. He tensed, expecting a last minute accusation.

"I think it's time that we discussed Cassia's prospects for marriage," Caecilia said pointedly to her husband. Cassia's joyful whoop was the last sound he heard as he walked away. Somehow it set everything right.

Chapter Two

Roman Spies Tell No Lies

Rome — Palatine Hill, a few weeks later

"And what have you to tell us, boy?" Emperor Maxentius addressed the nervous young army officer. A patrician with an easy future, Legionary Tribune Titus Fabius Titianus stood at attention before him. Maxentius sat at his desk with his arms folded expectantly. General Ruricius Pompeianus and a small gathering of priests and officers were with Maxentius in his private study, which served as his war room. They all waited for the tribune to give his report.

"The details have taken time to reach us, but our spies say Constantine's son was in Ariminum living with a pleb[5] gold merchant and his family. He has not been in contact with his father or any other member of his family as far as we can tell, sir. We think he may be headed further east on a trading ship."

"And what of Constantine? Has he made any attempts to find the boy himself?" Maxentius tossed his feet up onto the edge of the desk. The red leather

---

[5] Short for plebian, Roman person of middle-class origin, some of these families were as rich and powerful as the nobility

boots worn only by the men who ruled Rome were new, the leather still supple as Maxentius absently brushed dirt from them.

"None that we know of sir," Titus said.

Maxentius dropped his feet and spoke quickly to those assembled around him. "Constantine knows his response to his son's attack on my sister exposes a weakness, and he's made it a point to keep Fausta in the dark. She writes that he tells her victory is at hand and nothing else." He jumped up from his chair and paced anxiously back and forth across the marble floor. His frustration, held in check until then, reached the breaking point.

"Gods, this is maddening! What can be done? Fausta knows nothing, my so-called informers know nothing, and you slugs know nothing! Why do I bother keeping any of you alive!" He scanned the stern faces around him, young and old men both, in heavy black robes. The men glared back at him. As one, they turned to Ruricius, who was his Praetorian Prefect and should handle his outburst. To his credit, Ruricius did not look away. Instead he too glared, daring them to find fault with his friend and emperor. Most of the men shied away under his withering scrutiny.

One, however, did not.

He was Servius Caepionis, the Flamen Dialis, the high priest of Jupiter. He was annoyed at the summons, but when Maxentius pressed for a meeting with all the flamines, he had no choice but to comply. Such conclaves were becoming more frequent as the war stretched on. Now that his father Maximian was dead, Maxentius relied on the flamines' counsel and that of his generals. It was often a thankless job, and the flamines plotted ways to undermine each other almost as much as they plotted against Constantine. Servius was one of the few who was more than just a sanctimonious politician; he genuinely had some experience with battle and how to win in the high games of war.

Before he took on his permanent role as the Flamen Dialis, Servius had served in the military under Maximian for many years. He was a brilliant strategist who now spoke quietly to his chief. "Maxentius, why risk Crispus reuniting with his father? Send someone to kill the boy and the problem is solved."

Maxentius whirled around to face him. His voice was thick with sarcasm. "Just kill him? Excellent notion! Just how do you propose I do that without Constantine using it against me?"

Servius disregarded Maxentius' rudeness. "Don't send idiots or slaves. In fact, I know just the man, a Teuton. He's quick, and he's clean. It will never come back to you."

"Surely you are not speaking of Charietto?" asked Lucius Scipio, the Flamen Quirinalis. As the high priest of Quirinus, he was the most junior flamen in attendance. He was a quiet man and only spoke when he truly had something to say.

"The same, do you object?"

Lucius was blunt. "Of course I do. The man is a savage. Neither quick nor clean, if you ask me. To employ such a dishonest rascal is absurd. He will kill everyone in the household and leave a trail of blood straight back to the emperor. Only a fool would trust him."

Ruricius bristled at that. He had used the

man's services himself. "Lucius, your past with the man is coloring your judgment. The incident you speak of was long ago, and in fairness you forced Charietto's hand. Notwithstanding that one messy episode with your cousin's murderer, he has been very useful. "

Maxentius quieted them both, saying, "If Ruricius says he is acceptable, then I believe it. Send word to the man. Tell him his emperor wants Crispus' head in his hands by the new moon, and I don't care how, so long as the deed does not come back to me."

"What else?" Maxentius asked Titus, moving on before Lucius could stir up more controversy.

Young Titus continued. "Tribune Firmilianus sends word from Judea. Constantine's mother Helena has disappeared. She was last seen with Macarius, apparently a well-placed Jew and a man of good repute, even here in Rome. There are rumors of some mysterious find, a sacred artifact of great power she uncovered in Aelia Capitolina[6]. However, she and her people eluded our spies and have not been seen in some weeks. Some say she left for Armenia, to the court of Tiridates."

Servius shook his head. "Eluded by an old woman, what manner of spy are we employing? This could be important and a more senior man needs to be in charge. From what I have heard, she left on a religious pilgrimage of some sort. She's probably found a Christian relic of some sort, probably something claimed sacred, that would make sense."

"She did, and it is, sir. That much we can

---

[6] Name for Jerusalem after the sack of 70 AD when it became a Roman colony

confirm. She visited locations revered to Christians. Nothing was amiss, we were merely keeping track of her, and then she went missing suddenly. Later we heard a rumor that her people found a miraculum hidden in a cave. The exact nature of what she found, we do not know but we have suspicions."

"And?" Servius said, irritation beginning to show on his bearded face.

"And, sir? We do not know, as I said..."

"The suspicions, fool. What does Firmilianus think she has found?" Servius spat, losing his battle to be patient with the man.

"He thinks it's a cruxifix sir. Or at least pieces of one. Perhaps the same one the Christians believe their carpenter god died upon."

"A cross?" Ruricius added with a laugh. "You're afraid of a cross? Why do we concern ourselves with a piece of wood?"

"Do not mock the gods!" Maxentius said sharply. "You lack understanding of deep matters, Ruricius. These Christians are a strange lot. We have no idea what powers are at work here so someone had best find out."

He turned to his tribune. "Titus, I want you to oversee this Judean business. Send reliable people this time. I want to know what it is Helena has found in that wasteland, and where she is. If she has gone to Armenia, then lean on our friend Maximinus Daia to keep her there. That part of the world is still under his thumb."

To Ruricius he said, "And you see to this matter of Constantine's son as a priority. Hire this Teton you and Servius speak so highly about at once."

Titus and Ruricius stood to leave, but Maxentius stopped them. Servius was leaving too, but he stopped as well, although he was ready to go.

"Not yet, Ruricius. What news on Verona? It's crucial we hold the city. How many legions did the levies on Aquileia and Patavium bring?"

"They have sent only half a legion each, but it is no matter. The city is easy to defend sitting as it does in the loop of the River Adige. Its fortifications are intact, and the people are firmly in our camp. We can hold it."

"See that you do, Ruricius. That defeat at Brixia was shameful. The consequences of failing again would see your reputation suffer beyond repair and Rome at the full mercy of Constantine," Maxentius said. The prior year in Brixia, Constantine had slaughtered Ruricius' men and sent his army into full retreat. By the time Ruricius regained order, the battle was over, and the day belonged to Constantine. Ruricius was still horribly embarrassed about it. Everyone knew he had been eager for an opportunity to restore his honor ever since.

Ruricius stood at attention. "No, I will not disappoint you, my lord. I swear it!" Determination burned on his face.

Maxentius nodded, "See that you don't." To the group he said, "I have complete faith in General Ruricius. We shall prove to Constantine that he does not face cowards here."

Servius, the naysayer rejoined the debate. "In case the opposite is true, we need to be able to defend Rome if Constantine penetrates this far south. You'll have to leave several legions behind to defend it. At all costs, Constantine must not take Rome," said

Servius in the tone of a former soldier with much blood on his hands. "In a civil war, the people side with victors, not the vanquished. They will hand the city to Constantine along with your head."

"Constantine cannot attack if he cannot get to us," Maxentius said in a rare moment of brilliance. "We'll tear down every bridge and leave an armed and mounted cohort at each road. If Constantine cannot even reach the city, he cannot possibly hope to take it. We held out in a siege before; we can do it again. While Constantine sits outside our walls, Maximinus Daia will arrive from the East to come to our aid, and we will trap him in between Daia's army and mine."

Even the naysayer Servius could not argue against the plan. "That just might work," he conceded.

Chapter Three

Croesus' Revenge

"And here she is…Croesus' Revenge is a good name for her, eh? The years have been hard on her but she's still a beauty," the captain said, pointing to an old fishing galley sitting low in the waters of the Adriatic Sea. The galley was a sad sight in the Ariminum seaport where newer, better-outfitted merchant ships and pleasure vessels were docked. Sagging masts with tattered sails edged in green and black mold decorated her deck. On her hull, the memory of blue paint appeared in scattered splotches, and what was once the graceful carving of a mermaid on the prow was now missing its tail and head. The shop sat low in the water, but that was not her fault; a cargo of gold bullion weighed her down. "She'll be on her way to Bithynia tomorrow. We never let her sit in port too long, or we'll have thieves nosing around her."

The Croesus' Revenge was a clever disguise for the shipments of gold into Ariminum. She was rickety enough that marauding pirates were apt to overlook her, so she usually went unmolested except for the occasional sea storm. The crew and a slew of well-armed brutes milled around the deck, waiting to head out to deeper waters. If not for them, Crispus might have wondered if the ship were even seaworthy at all.

"She…she's…um…extraordinary," Crispus said, struggling to find something good to say about it. He was overly generous, but it was unwise to make an enemy of the captain. The ship's owner was a fellow gold trader, Publius Julianus, who promised loyalty and discretion in his men, but with his life in the balance Crispus was taking no chances. The captain escorted Crispus around the ship and below deck to his quarters. However humble, it was evidently a much coveted space. When Crispus returned to the open air, he caught angry stares from the displaced occupants of the berth.

On the main deck preparations were completed. The ship was ready to leave, but they remained in the port. Crispus could not imagine why, and when the ship was still in place hours later, he was even more troubled. He soon learned his fears were well founded. He watched in utter disbelief as Cassia and her attendants made their way across the footbridge and onto the Croesus' Revenge. Guards who stayed close accompanied her, yet she had many friends among the rough crew if her warm greetings and smile were any indication. As she moved among them with ease, Crispus could not help wondering how many of them she had bedded.

"She's making the rounds I suppose," he mumbled spitefully.

A quick interrogation of the captain yielded the truth. Cassia was to accompany the ship all the way to Nicomedia. Somehow, she managed to convince her father a few weeks abroad would be good for her. It was all nonsense, of course. Crispus knew if he had not been on the ship neither would she, and he wanted no part of whatever game she was playing.

He leaned against the vessel's railing, quietly taking in the comedy of Cassia parading herself. Soon, he became aware that she knew he watched her. Worse, she misinterpreted his gaze. Her lips widened in a coy smirk, and her strutting around the men took a more brazen turn. Crispus was embarrassed for her. If she knew how pathetically foolish she looked...but, he left the thought unfinished. His mind drifted again to Nicomedia with a heartfelt wish to see Julia who was a different sort of girl.

Julia – just her name brought both pleasure and pain. Crispus stood with the wind behind him and Cassia's piercing laughter in his ear. Still, he was deaf to all except the memory of Julia's sobbing the last time they were together. It had been three years since he told her his father was sending him to command the Rhine frontier. So much of what had happened since then was rooted in that night. He wished he could forget it, but the memory remained firmly stuck in his mind, a sliver of regret that still stung despite his denials. Crispus was so occupied by the endless battles he fought over his feelings for Julia that he failed to notice a man had joined him at the railing.

"Ho there! We were supposed to be in the East another two weeks, but Cassius summons us early. Are you the urgent cause to which we owe this felicitas?"

Crispus whirled around at the sound to find he stared into a great hairy chest the color of bronze and just as solid. He took a step back to look the person in the eye; he refused to be cowed by a nosy stranger. Standing before him blocking the sun was a middle-aged titan with skin like sunbaked leather. His bulging muscles hinted at violence, but his eyes were gentle ebony pits that matched Crispus' gaze in intensity. There was a hard moment of silence between them before the giant's face softened. He laughed and clapped a monstrous hand across Crispus' shoulder. Crispus shifted uncomfortably under the weight of it.

"Your pardon! I didn't mean to startle you." The man's face broke into the wide grin found in men with natural confidence. "My name is Donatus, friend. Donatus Magnas of Casae Nigra. You must be someone very important, or very rich. Julianus never uses new men for an important run like this, and I know every soul on this ship except you. Doesn't seem that you really belong here, does it?"

Crispus angrily pushed the man's arm away. Undaunted, Donatus tried again but kept his hands to himself this time. "Come now, I'm only joking with you. It's a long voyage." Donatus lowered his voice. "I might be a good man for you to know. What's your name, stranger?"

Crispus looked up at the man, irritation plain on his face. "You're better off not knowing my name Donatus Magnas of Casae Nigra," he said with a hint of sarcasm at the title. "My business onboard this ship is none of your affair."

"Unfriendly still? Well, have it your way then. But see that fellow over there, the skinny one with the rusty dagger? Take a good look at it. You may find it in your back one of these nights. That's Tobias, Publius' brother-in-law, and those men behind him are his little followers, more like lovers from the way they fawn over him. He's convinced you're the runaway prince the soldiers have been looking for and the only thing standing in the way of him pressing the matter is me. Do you want my help or not, because you are in dangerous waters in more ways than one."

The stranger had a point. Crispus looked over his shoulder at the crew watching him with distrustful eyes. Who would be the first to try him? They all seemed to be waiting for Donatus to make a decision. Crispus chose his next words carefully. "My name is Valerius, and I am not this wealthy prince you lot think I am. I'm visiting friends in Nicomedia and my presence on this ship is a favor to erase a debt, nothing more."

Donatus stretched out his hand to Crispus. He gave a deep and rumbling laugh. "That's a good joke, sir!" He lowered his voice. "I know who you are. I recognize your features. You're one of the Constantii – a son or grandson if I were to hazard a guess." Donatus' nod registered the surprise on Crispus' face as confirmation, but he did not need it.

"When I was not much older than you, I fought under General Constantius against Carausius. His blood runs in your veins as sure as I am standing here. It's your eyes that give you away. They're like two rising moons set in a stone-hard face. Never saw anybody with eyes like that except in your family." He stopped talking in a moment of quiet memory before he finished his thought.

"Constantius was the best commander I ever knew. He was truly a father to us. I would see no harm come to any in his bloodline."

Crispus decided to give up his lie. Sticking to it was likely to cause more harm than good. It was obvious this man knew his family. "Yes, Constantius was my grandfather. My father is Constantine, his first born. And I am Constantine's first son. I haven't been on this ship an hour and already I'm revealed? Who else served under my family here?" Crispus asked him, dreading the answer.

"Only me." Donatus assured him. He moved a few respectful steps back from Crispus, still out of the earshot of the crew. "You may rely on me, sir. I left your grandfather's service chasing a woman I never caught, and I have regretted it ever since. Allow me to fulfill my Sacramentum in your service. If you give me this chance to redeem my honor I will not fail you."

"I appreciate your discretion, and thank you for the offer but I have strong forces against me, I can't in good conscience make you a party to my troubles. Excuse me, I need to leave." Crispus told him, as tactfully as possible given that the secrets Donatus held. He was tired of talking to the stranger, however kind and well-meaning, and of Cassia's whirligig with the crew; he watched while she went below with one of them. Suddenly nauseated, he turned to go to his own quarters.

"As you say, but I am your man nonetheless!" Donatus shouted at his back, undeterred by Crispus' cold reception. He issued another laugh that followed Crispus below deck, past the room where loud moans within told him Cassia was already occupied with her cabin boy. The sound of Cassia's lovemaking changed his mind. Who knew what she would tell her ruffians about him during her bed talk? Crispus beat a hasty retreat back to Donatus, who still stood at the deck railing.

"Sup with me tonight," Crispus said without preamble. "Afterward, if you still want to serve me, I'll tell you my story."

Donatus nodded, then chuckled, "I hope you have better rations than the cook's onion's soup."

"You're in luck, Donatus, it so happens I do." He clapped him on the shoulder, thinking of the supplies Marcus Cassia sent for his journey.

That night over a satisfying meal of salted pork, bread and hard cheese, Crispus and Donatus talked for hours. Donatus told him how he came to be on Croesus's Revenge. He was a Berber by birth, from the African province of Zeugitana. His father was a prosperous ivory trader whose greed and recklessness eventually led him into poverty. As a last resort to restore his fortunes, he gave away Donatus to his Roman neighbors, the Julianii. The family had been gold merchants for generations and Donatus found himself placed as a bodyguard to Publius Julianus, the eldest son. It was a crushing blow for Donatus, being reduced to the status of a servant, but he came with Publius when he took charge of Croesus's Revenge and rose to become first officer. He was the most feared man on the ship, and the only reason Crispus could sleep without fearing a knife at his throat.

Donatus and Crispus swapped stories of their disappointing fathers, bonding to each other in the ship's hold as they ate their fill of Crispus' private supplies.

"I am glad I am not more like my father," Crispus said. He is a stubborn man, but also blind and foolish. He swallowed Fausta's story without so much as a question whispered in my direction, and I will never forgive him for it."

Donatus was firm but gentle. "But you must forgive. Otherwise, how can you expect forgiveness in return? Surely you made mistakes as well, and only by confessing and renouncing them can you become whole again."

There was something familiar about Donatus' words. "I hear my grandmother's voice in your words. You're a Christian?"

"Would it surprise you if I were?"

Crispus shrugged. "No, I suppose not. Are there others among the crew?"

"Many. All of them are former soldiers who have shed blood for Rome. Publius Julianus only hires the most reliable men for his gold shipments. We are all part of the same fellowship. Publius and his family are also converts. We have been blessed to feed so many from the bread of life."

Crispus interrupted him. "Perhaps, but I was raised with Roman gods as well. So what I do know is that the two do not mix, and there is no way around it. I find it best just to leave the matter alone."

Crispus yawned. "It's late. I should turn in. I'm glad to have met you Donatus." After their goodnights, he left Donatus in the hold of the ship, surrounded by barrels of pickled eggs and a few amphorae of wine, and went to find his bed.

Crispus settled into the uncomfortable straw bedding of his little sleeping berth with a tired sigh. There was barely enough room to roll over in it. Crispus tossed about for hours before he could settle into sleep. When he did, he had vivid dreams of Nicomedia again. At the center of them was Julia, as always. When he awoke, he lay very still for a long time, recalling the first time he laid eyes on her.

He was twelve years old that year and wintering in Emperor Diocletian's court in Nicomedia for the second year in a row. It was during the feast to mark Diocletian's 55th birthday that Crispus first met Julia Galeria Valerius, Diocletian's only grandchild.

Crispus and Licinius were at the back of the feasting hall where the guests with no money and just a few connections, were confined away from the guests of proper lineage. They were desperate to avoid the eagle eyes of Constantia, Licinius' mother and Crispus' least favorite aunt, and she had an unnerving habit of turning up just when they thought they had eluded her.

Licinius nudged Crispus and pointed to the front of the room, to a small circle of couches where court officials and foreign emissaries gathered around Diocletian. As the aged emperor droned on about his past glories, there sat Julia directly behind him on a small couch of her own, making faces and mocking every word. It was reckless and rude and exactly what Crispus and his cousin would do themselves if they could. The boys were immediately captivated by her. Here was a girl who knew how to have fun.

After a few minutes, she noticed them watching and came over to them. Up close, she took Crispus' breath away. She was tall for her age, with hair the same golden brown color as his mother's and she had plenty of it. It fell in wave after wave down her back, nearly to her waist. Her almond-shaped eyes were a warm shade of amber with flecks of gold and set wide apart above high cheekbones and full, pouty lips. Crispus could barely look at her without blushing deep red.

"Salve' boys, that was something wasn't it?"
She laughed in a high, clear voice that was sweet as
music to Crispus.

"Forgive us, but who are you, girl?" said
Licinius in a tone that made it seem as though he
could not possibly care any less. He made his voice
deep, straightened his tunic, and was as intimidating
as he could manage on the spot.

Crispus shook his head in disgust. "You know
who she is, idiot! She's in the emperor's family,
otherwise she wouldn't be so close to him."

Licinius reddened. He dropped his shoulders
and shot Crispus a warning look. "I know that, of
course. I meant what is her name?"

He turned to Julia. "I'm Licinius the younger,
son of the same, and this is Crispus. Emperor
Constantius is our grandfather. Crispus is not counted
with the rest of the family though. We count him with
the livestock and slaves."

"He lies. Pay him no mind. What do they call
you?" Crispus asked.

"Julia Galeria. Emperor Diocletian is my
grandfather. I'm pleased to make your acquaintance."
She leaned closer to them and lowered her voice, a
conspirator sharing secrets. "Listen boys, I know
where the cook keeps the Faustian Falerian. Have you
ever had any? It's divine!"

Falerian wine? Both boys shook their heads.
No one had ever offered them wine, especially not an
imperial daughter. They hesitated.

Julia smiled broadly. "Well, do you want to? I
saw the cook bring it in this morning, but I don't
want to try it alone. Will you come with me?" She
swallowed hard against a visible lump of excitement

in her throat. "Say yes, please!"

Crispus and Licinius grinned at each other. Faustian Falerian was the best wine in the whole world. Crispus and Licinius heard it mentioned more than once over the years. What could it hurt too see why there was so much fuss over it? They looked around for Constantia. She had her back to them, laughing in the corner with her mother, Flavia. The boys followed like sheep as Julia led the way down to the kitchens and through a wide doorway into the cool damp of the cellar.

She pointed to a small wooden barrel in the corner. "The Faustian," she announced proudly.

Crispus and Licinius stood slack-jawed as dolts. Julia pushed them hard from behind. "Oh, for heaven's sake! Find something we can pour it into." She ran back to the door. "Hurry, I'll stand guard."

Crispus punched Licinius in the arm. "Come on cousin! Help me before we get caught!"

They quickly found an empty storage jar and filled it to nearly overflowing with the wine. As they ran from the cellar with their stolen booty in hand, they inadvertently left a trail of spilled wine and wet footsteps behind them.

Crispus' grandmother Helena happened along in time to see them disappear around a corner. Spotting the evidence, she followed the trail to Julia's room. There she found the three of them huddled around the jar taking turns gulping it down. Her wrath was immediate, severe and directed at Julia, in particular.

"Julia Galeria! This is a fine way for a noble girl to behave, hiding in closed rooms and drinking wine with boys! You wicked child! In another time and place, your father would have you killed for this!" Helena swung at Julia's face with a light rebuking slap, that inflicted no real harm; she was after all Diocletian's grandchild. Crispus and Licinius both watched with renewed respect for the Helena. It was plain that she was not a woman to trifle with at all.

Julia stood in shock; angry tears welled in her eyes. She put her hand to her cheek to check for imaginary injuries. Crispus and Licinius stood behind her, quietly. For an instant, Julia looked ready to break under Helena's withering condemnation. Then she remembered herself. She regained her composure to match Helena's iron gaze with one of her own.

"I'm responsible, that's true. Since you have punished me, let them go. Otherwise, my father and grandfather will hear of what you did to me."

"Are you threatening me, girl? I am not frightened of your father or your grandfather."

"It's not a threat. It is just a plain fact. Lay hands on me again and that's exactly what I will do." Julia said with all her courage before she left the room, leaving Helena and the boys looking after her.

That was the first time Julia saved Crispus, but it would not be the last. As Crispus lay in his humble bunk envisioning her as a young girl, he realized she stood between him and some well-deserved punishment more times than he could count. As he drifted off to sleep he felt a twinge of guilt and an even stronger longing to see her again.

The next two weeks on board the Croesus' Revenge brought nothing but difficulties for Crispus. Assailed on two fronts, he could find no rest. During the nights, he had to contend with Cassia's unwanted advances, and during the day, the wary eyes of the crew followed him everywhere.

And, of course, an attack on him did come, when he was least expecting it – and from an equally unexpected source – Rubio, an unassuming slave boy Cassia used to carry love notes to Crispus. Crispus thought him harmless and shooed him away every time she sent him. Because of that, the night Crispus was attacked, he thought nothing of Rubio's presence at his door.

"Tell her no. And trouble me no more," Crispus told him after reading the latest note from Cassia. As Crispus was turning away for the umpteenth time, the boy took a wild lunge at him with a razor-sharp dagger he had concealed behind him.

Crispus deflected the blow easily, spinning the blade from Rubio's grasp and turning it to press it into the tender flesh below the boy's dimpled chin. A single red bead formed where the point met flesh. Crispus pressed harder, widening it.

"Foolish boy! Were you but a few years older, I would kill you where you stand!" Crispus tightened his grip on the boy.

Rubio gasped in pain. "Please, I beg you –" The boy's terrified voice went hoarse, little more than a whisper.

Crispus made no reply. He drew back his arm to slice the boy's throat, but then stopped as if restrained by invisible hands.

"I cannot do it," he said at last. He dropped his sword hand to his side. The boy collapsed against the corridor wall. Tears of gratitude rolled down his cheeks while his hands slid down inside his tunic as he pulled at the sagging garment. A glint of steel flashed, and Crispus felt a sharp pain in his groin as another of the boy's secreted weapons found its mark.

"You mad dog!" Crispus shouted. He swiped at the boy with the dagger, but Rubio scurried out of reach. Crispus gave chase down the passageway but stopped when he felt the breeze from yet another blade as it sliced the air near his ear. Another man joined Rubio's assault, a giant beast hidden in the shadows. His menacing form filled the hallway, but his size was of no consequence. It was the jagged sword he carried and the quick, bloody death lurking behind his eyes that gave Crispus courage. Crispus steadied himself with his own dagger poised to strike. *Let my aim be true,* he prayed to any god listening.

Dodging to the side to avoid the man's move on him, Crispus buried his blade deep into the giant's chest. With a guttural cry, the man wrenched the blade from his body in one fluid motion and made to slice Crispus with it. When the awkward blow came, it missed Crispus' head and lodged in the plank wall next to him instead. Seizing the advantage, Crispus slashed at his assailant's arms and face with his own blade, forcing a retreat and staying clear of the man's weapon.

With his enemy faltering, Crispus pressed his attack but had to give way again when Rubio intervened in the struggle. The boy jumped on his back, choking him. Crispus struggled to dislodge the boy while the giant man collected his knife and slashed at him afresh. Crispus felt blood running down his side, and the pressure of Rubio's arm locked around his neck threatened to strangle him.

I cannot die this way! He rallied for a moment,

but his vision was dimming. Though he was strong, he was nearly unconscious.

What happened next defied logic; had to be a hallucination from lack of air. From nowhere, Donatus appeared in the fray. He crashed headlong into Crispus' assailant, causing him to drop his weapon and fall hard against the wall. The men grappled with each other, locked in mortal combat, but Donatus managed to gain the advantage. Rubio lost his grip on Crispus' neck when Donatus snatched the other man away. Crispus seized the boy and flung him hard away from him. Rubio hit the wall with a sickening thud that left him dazed on the floor.

Donatus was not finished with his man yet. He grabbed the stranger's head and rammed it into the wall. Wood splintered in all directions. Throwing the struggling man to the ground, he proceeded to stomp and stab the life out of him. Crispus watched as each blow fell until the deed was done and Donatus stood panting before him.

"No harm will come to you while I breathe," he swore again to Crispus.

Rubio had seen enough. He was no longer the crafty knifeman. He was again the frightened child, crying and wanting to flee. Crispus' hard grip stopped him.

"Please, I had no choice! They made me do it! He promised to throw me overboard! He swore he would –"

"Quiet now. Your life is still your own. This is in your mistress' hands. You can explain it to her."

"Explain what to me? What happened here?" Cassia appeared at the end of the hallway and came to them. Donatus moved to restrain her, but she pushed him away. Hard on her heels, others began arriving so that the small space soon filled with crew members, including the captain and his most trusted men. In an instant, Rubio was in shackles. His accomplice was less fortunate. His battered body was flung far out into the churning waters of the Adriatic as food for the fishes. There were heavy accusations back and forth between the crew, but none came from Cassia. Her feigned shock appeared real as she clutched at Crispus, sobbing pleas of innocence.

"I would not! I could not, not ever. I would never harm you. I – I love you. Please, you must believe me!" she pleaded. "I just told him to deliver a message. I swear I did not send him to harm you!"

Crispus' anger dimmed at her obvious distress. He removed her arms from around his neck and was gentler with her than he had intended.

"But he did try for my life just the same." Crispus said quietly, needing her to understand him well. "I want to know why though I can guess the truth died with him" he said, pointing to the dead man sprawled out before them. "He probably heard about the prize on my head and enlisted this boy here to help him."

A trail of tears slid down Cassia's face. Crispus held his ground in the face of it. "Now you manufacture tears?" he asked softly. "Do you understand that you put my life at risk. Should I now be grateful you feel some shame?"

Cassia opened her mouth to speak, to find some mitigating words, but they escaped her. Crispus' eyes upon hers were hard, his face set against her.

Conceding her defeat, she simpered, "Is there is nothing I can say that you will believe?"

"No, there is no lie you can tell that will matter now. The best thing you can do is leave. Now. Go back to your quarters and do no bother me further." The ice in his voice permitted no response. She turned to leave, anger and hurt plain on her face. Crispus avoided her eyes. Instead, he turned to Donatus, his savior. Donatus was soaked in sweat and his chest heaved from exertion.

"My oath stands. I promise to guard your back, make your enemies mine and fight by your side now and always." he told Crispus in solemn resolve.

Crispus studied him for a time, considering the pledge. It was no light matter to hold a loyalty obligation with a dangerous man and so Crispus did it with care. "I accept your vow and make one of my own to you. I promise to never give you cause to regret it or any reason to break it." Crispus held out his hand. Donatus took it though his was still bloody from his fight with the slain man. Crispus looked down at the gore that now covered both their hands and nodded in approval.

"Sealed in the shed blood between us." Donatus said in approval.

Crispus issued him his first orders. "Keep watch outside my door, and let none pass you alive." Donatus was happy to comply. With Donatus posted faithfully nearby, at last Crispus could rest without fearing another attack. For the first time in weeks, he slept soundly.

For the remaining days at sea, Crispus kept to himself and avoided Cassia as he would death or the plague. She was both to him, but without her family connections he would have a difficult time reaching the safety of Nicomedia. Cassia knew it as well as he did which complicated matters. Before long he would have to come to her and she set about making sure he knew it in the most overt ways possible. More than once, he had come upon her making tearful, angry complaints about him to the crew, her attendants and the captain as well. The others suffered to listen to her, but the captain appeared to wish to be anywhere else other than listening to his friend's spoiled daughter whine about his houseguest.

Unable to make sense of Cassia or anything she did, Crispus at last went to Donatus about her. "Women and their whims!" he moaned. "Cassia has the gall to expect an apology from me. She will never get it! I don't know why she cares so much. It's not as though she suffers from a lack of attention."

Donatus had watched them in bemused silence for days without offering his opinion. Now he hardly knew where to begin.

"Crispus, you must surely be blind! Can you not see the girl is in love with you? Since she boarded this ship she has been trying to get you to feel something for her, even if it is anger. If you indulge her in anyway, you will never be rid of her."

"And there's the trouble. I need her help once we leave this ship. Her father promised me safe passage to Nicomedia."

"Did he? Then perhaps that's something you should consider more than your feelings. If you need her, you'll have to yield to her in some way. If not, then you'll have to make your own way to Nicomedia. I could help get you to Nicomedia safety, but you must decide – trust me or appease Cassia."

As if there was a real choice to make, "You, of course!" Crispus chuckled at the irony of his dealings with Cassia, after the debacle with Fausta. "The sooner I get away from Cassia, the better I'll feel about everything that has happened and everything that is to come."

Chapter Four

Linus of Ephesus

"Terra Firma!"

The bellow of the watchman woke Crispus from a restless sleep. Rising from his bunk, he peered out the porthole. Across the expanse of sapphire blue sea were the lands the Romans called Anatolia, in all their splendor. The port city Ephesus served for a shining invitation to travelers near and far to sample her delights before moving on to an even richer land, the rare beauty of the crown jewel, the capital Nicomedia.

There Crispus would find rest there and a respite from the burdens of Constantine's wrath. His father's anger followed him like some ferocious monster devouring everything in its wake. He doubted Rubio or his dead assailant would have moved against him unless driven by the promise of the emperor's price on his son's head.

"What if Donatus had not appeared to help me?" Crispus mused. "I would be dead right now. And that assault was Cassia's fault as well, whether that was her intent or not."

The debate that had waged inside him for days now drew to a swift close as Crispus found his righteous anger at Cassia again. "She won't get an apology from me, whatever the cost. I'll take my chances with Donatus!"

Accepting Donatus' help him was the wisest thing he could have done for himself. The giant was meticulous about his loyalty and his promises. He vowed to help and he did, appearing beside Crispus early in the morning. He announced his plans to go into the city ahead of him to find safe passage to Nicomedia for both of them. He was leaving his appointment on Croesus' Revenge and had already informed the captain. Donatus was ready to throw in his lot with Crispus and if he could not find passage for them, they would simply take to the open road together. When Donatus left on his mission, Crispus could only feel grateful to have a man like Donatus at his side, whatever the outcome of their plans.

It was a pleasure to place the turbulent days aboard Croesus's Revenge behind him, particularly when the ripe fruit of the Ephesian port dangled before his eyes in the glory of the morning. Like all sea-faring cities, there was something mystical about the pristine seas and green landscape, teeming with life overflowing. The rolling waves and fresh, salty breeze washed away the grime of the night.

Ephesus was famous for its vibrant, if sordid nighttime pursuits. Every corruption imaginable was available, for a price. The business of pleasure was more inconspicuous further from the port, in the pricier brothels that resembled fine houses. Here at the water's edge, vice flourished in explicit ways in the backrooms of uncared-for insulae and tight alleyways. Daylight hours were to count nighttime profits, and decent citizens fled the city's port at dusk for this very reason.

Crispus watched from the deck as a small army of hired swordsmen gathered to oversee the unloading of the vessel. The crew began to carry out the strongboxes, one after another. With so much cargo on display, a hostile crowd of dirty, bedraggled loiterers gathered to watch and call out raucous jeers to the men who responded with curses of their own. It was an opportune distraction that allowed Crispus to slip unnoticed from the ship.

The Via Arcadiana was the wide central street that led from the harbor into the city proper. Crispus ventured down it and tried not to question the wisdom of abandoning the plans already in place for him. He took in the sights of the city. All around him were trade shops and public buildings clustered around the vast open marketplace. As Crispus walked along he paused to notice some of the bath houses and drinking holes, but it was the more carnal offerings that drew his attention.

He recalled fondly long ago when he was a boy spending time with his father. Constantine personally took Crispus to visit his first brothel when he came of age, waiting outside the gilded doors with a stern face and brooking no fearful dissuasion from Crispus. When the deed was done, he took Crispus not to the palace complex where he could clean up alone, but to the public bathhouse with the other soldiers. Crispus felt like one of them. He remembered the day as a cherished memory that was now bittersweet.

Crispus wandered the streets of Ephesus aimlessly, his thoughts clouded with visions of the past, and of his father. When that became too much for him, he ducked into the first taberna that felt welcoming to his black mood. Several hours later, nightfall found him in the same establishment with a cup of wine and a half-eaten bowl of rabbit stew in front of him. Crispus sat alone staring into the distance, his mood as dark as the shadowy inn. His mind worked furiously to cobble together a reason not to throw himself into the sea and be done with it. The whole business of living past his mistakes and missed opportunities was miserable to contemplate. His shoulders slumped over his wine. Even the whores milling about gave him a wide berth, which did not help his mood. He picked up his cup, drained it and called for another.

The mad plan he and Donatus put together on the ship that morning would unravel if his instincts about the man were wrong. He relied on them, they were always accurate, but nothing ever happens for the first time, until it does. Donatus had come into the city ahead of him but what if he did not return? Crispus quieted the internal voices of doubt with a reminder that Donatus had already saved his life once. There was no reason to think he would not do it again.

The chaotic musings of escaping to Nicomedia brought his beloved Viatoro to the forefront of his mind. He had not considered how he would retrieve him now that he had arrived in the city without Cassius' friendship. Cassius sent Viatoro by a faster route than Crispus. He should be in Ephesus already but Crispus would have to seek out the horse trader Josephus himself and risk discovery.

"It would seem that I have to apologize to Cassia after all, if I want to see Viatoro again." Crispus muttered in resignation. His lips curled in distaste at the bitter draught of having to crawl back to Cassia for help.

Just then, a hulking figure appeared in the open doorway of the taberna. The man was so large he filled it completely. Crispus knew before he moved any closer that it was Donatus. He breathed a sigh of relief. Donatus found him right away. He strode over to where Crispus sat filled with something closer to cheer now that his way to Nicomedia had arrived.

"I never doubted you for a moment." Crispus told him and pretended it was true.

"At last I find you. I did not know there were so many inns and tabernae in Ephesus! It has changed since I was last here. I dare say I have been in twenty of them looking for you, and now I find you drunk and downcast. Come, lay one of your worries aside, I have made arrangements for us."

"Excellent!" Crispus said, genuine in his happiness. He was impressed with Donatus' resourcefulness, and he was grateful to avoid Cassia. "I trust you did not reveal my name?"

There was an embarrassing pause, then a sheepish Donatus admitted, "Well, I had no choice. But where I take you, you will have friends. I found the location of your horse Viatoro as well. He's in a public stable, but he is waiting for you as well. Trust me now and come with me."

Crispus did not bother to argue. He shrugged; he was a fugitive, after all. "Lead the way, my friend."

Outside the inn, Marble Street lay before them. Branching off from it was a labyrinth of cobblestoned side alleys and back streets. Crispus and Donatus walked just out of easy view of the light spilling from the open doorways lining the route.

They were close enough for the women standing inside them to beckon with lewd suggestions. Seeing a fresh faces excited them. Some of the more brazen even tried to pull Crispus inside the dingy walls of their keep. They ceased their efforts, however, when Donatus met the venture with an angry sneer, his blade at the ready. It seemed to Crispus that they walked endlessly, but at last Donatus stopped somewhere on the edge of a well-kept marketplace. Crispus came to stand beside him.

"Now we wait," Donatus said.

"Wait for whom? Who offers us aid?" Crispus asked warily.

Donatus did not answer. Crispus searched around him, seeking his answers in the light of the street lamps that lined the way. They blazed forth, glowing glass cylinders atop wrought iron poles. They had a radiance that was simply beautiful and nothing like Crispus had ever seen before. He had heard tales about the splendid streetlights of Ephesus[8] but the experience of the lamps revealing his way to safety was quite different, an unexpected joy.

Before him lay a small plaza formed by the city's Mithridates gate. It bordered the agora and the end of Marble Street with its assortment of gaming and pleasure houses, and a tall marble building that formed the apex of the arrangement. The design of the plaza was such that the wide stone steps of the building formed a natural platform. It was easy to imagine the area as it would be in the morning, filled

---

[8] One of only three streets in the world with streetlights, Ephesus was possibly the first city to have them.

with newsreaders and street performers vying for the attentions of the rabble.

"This is the perfect place for a meeting. No one will expect you to hide in plain sight," Donatus said.

He gestured to the imposing structure in front of them. The Great Library of Celsus rose majestically against the night sky, illuminated from within by dozens of braziers kept aflame despite the late hour. The pale cream and sand-toned Phrygian marble appeared white against the background of the night sky. Four double rows of Corinthian styled columns lined the portico leading to three doors, the central of which was open to reveal the robed scholars scurrying back and forth, their arms full of scrolls. The columns were set together in groups of two and inside each stood a marble statue of a local god or goddess. Above them, on the second story of columns, statues of men in formal togas stood beside large rectangular windows like framed artwork. The entire façade was etched in intricate reliefs of intertwined flowers, grape vines and characters from Greek history: Bellerophon on Pegasus, Eros and Psyche and many others.

Crispus had never seen architecture quite like it. Not even the haughtiest buildings of Nicomedia could rival it for beauty or adherence to Roman engineering.

He nodded in appreciation. "Magnificent! I have heard it called a match for the Alexandria library, but I didn't credit it. I see now the praise is well-earned."

"The library is one of Ephesus' finest

achievements second only to the Artemision[9]." Donatus agreed.

Crispus clapped his friend on the shoulder. "You continue to surprise me Donatus. How do you know so much about Ephesian achievements? You're a man of many talents!"

"You forget, I was not always a rough solider, and we are more alike than you might think." Donatus told him shaking his head in quiet amusement.

As they approached the portico, Donatus stopped Crispus and moved forward alone. He searched around him, seeking someone or something among the columns. Crispus waited at the edge of the portico. He was nervous. He desperately wished that Donatus would hurry. It felt foolish to linger where there were learned men might recognize his face from coinage, regardless of disguise.

Crispus tried to put the troubling notion from his mind but he gazed again at the library. Under different circumstances, Crispus would have liked to venture inside the great library, to become lost amongst the Greek classics he loved as a child. An image of enjoying one of them with his mother came unbidden into his head. He could hear her soft, birdsong voice in his head. He pushed the memory away with regret; now was not the time for that kind of nostalgia. It was guaranteed only to vex him, clouding his judgment when he might need it.

"We should not lurk here among these

---

[9] Artemision - Greek temple dedicated to the goddess Artemis, one of the Seven Wonders of the Ancient World.

columns. It draws unnecessary suspicion. Did you not get some idea of when your man will appear – perhaps we arrived too early?" Crispus asked. Something was causing the back of his neck to prickle, but he could not place the source. His senses all aligned to search the darkness for a logical explanation for his dread – that he found none made it no better.

Donatus did not answer right away. Despite the cool night air, beads of sweat pooled at his temples. "This is the appointed hour. We will just have to be patient," he said with a shrug, but he had a cautious look as well.

Crispus frowned. "Donatus, I have followed you without complaint but my patience runs short when my life is in danger. Now please, tell me who are we meeting?" He kept his voice low, but his urgency was unmistakable.

Donatus surrendered the information to appease him and reassure himself, by the hopeful lilt in his voice. "We wait for a messenger from the house of Linus Pollio. The family are well-known Jews, but his branch of it quietly converted to Christianity some years ago. He's agreed to hide us and he retrieved your stallion for you. Well…I should say, he will hide *you*. I doubt he will offer me a place in the house, but the emperor's son can find houseroom."

"But I am neither Jew nor Christian. Why would he help me rather than turn me in for the reward? This could all be a trap, Donatus!" Crispus whispered, suddenly wondering at the wisdom of laying his life in Donatus' hands.

Donatus pointed to the worn stone steps

leading away from the portico. He leaned down to trace his finger along one stone, revealing the faint shape of a menorah scratched in crude letters along the side of one of them. "Do you see this? The Jews can be trusted with secrecy and discretion. It's been their way through a thousand years of people trying to kill them, and don't forget that many of the Christians are converted Jews who understand this. The man we are visiting is one of them. He won't allow any harm to come to us. His messenger promised to meet us at this spot as the second watch begins, and I have no doubt that is what will happen."

Crispus was incredulous at Donatus' naïveté. "So the only assurances we have that this man will not sell us to the highest bidder is his word as a converted Jew?"

"You will see," Donatus said simply.

While he was still speaking, a figure stepped from the shadows of the library. For a dizzying moment, Crispus thought the stranger a part of the array of stone gods clustered around them. The man wore a heavy woolen cloak with wide long sleeves. They rode high on his arms when he waved them forward, revealing a metal armband engraved with a small fish.

"As I promised..." Donatus said, breathing a little easier now that the messenger had arrived.

"Yes, but this story is unfinished. We must see where it leads. For both our sakes, I hope our trust in this man is not misplaced."

Donatus went to speak to the stranger. The two of them whispered together for some time before he returned to Crispus.

"He says we are to follow behind him and do

not stop no matter what happens along the way."

"As if we had a choice in the matter, Crispus muttered. He stilled the unrest in his heart and followed Donatus and the man from the marketplace.

Ephesus lay along straight lines that converged in the heart of the city where most of the residents lived. The trio walked eastward along Curetes Street, past the crumbling octagon that was the tomb of Arsinoe, the Egyptian princess exiled in Ephesus centuries ago. Crispus marked her tomb as a land feature to lead him back to the library should events at the house of Linus turn sour.

Crispus was apprehensive, but tried hard not to show it. As they went along, they reached a section of town where the houses were much nicer and sat on a gently sloping hill. When he thought he could endure no more suspense, they reached a gated wall set back a few paces from the street. The villa it enclosed was large but indistinct from the others around it. Along the perimeter, guards stood with daggers hanging at their waist and menace in their eyes. Inside the tall gates, Crispus could glimpse the layout of the villa. Its tiled roof divided large sections of stone and concrete, and its many windows were uncovered and brightly lit. Statues adorned the outer courtyard, and milling slaves were still at work keeping everything in good order.

The man leading them turned at last. He still had not given his name, but he ushered Crispus and Donatus inside the gate with an expectant nod at the guard. In short order, Crispus found himself in a large, well-appointed vestibule adorned with Christian symbols and a large altar placed along one wall. A heavyset man knelt before it, turned in profile to them. His hair was a mass of unruly curls, cut short in a trendy Roman style, and he wore flowing purple robes and fine leather sandals encrusted with jewels. The man sat unmoving, his hands clasped together in prayer. He sweated profusely, his face contoured with his efforts.

When at last the performance came to a merciful end, Linus stood to greet his guest. Crispus masked his impatience as he took the man's hands. To his disgust, Linus' palms were cold and sweat-soaked. Crispus resisted the urge to drop them, but he wiped his hands on his tunic in a casual way when they finished. Linus paid it no mind. His face contorted into a grin so wide, Crispus thought it might split into two. Try as he might, Crispus was too exhausted to return the affection, and he was not sure he wanted to now that he was here. There was something lurking beneath that grin that made him uncomfortable.

Donatus stayed behind in the vestibule, standing guard, tall and imposing by the doorway. Crispus felt better about being a stranger in a strange land with him at his back. The rest of the household immediately began to whisper about the visitors. Linus took Crispus into another room, the tablinum where he met with his clients.

The tablinum was an interesting space, with beautiful old frescos painted in a seldom used older style of gem-toned masonry blocks. The furnishings were the kind of tattered but once expensive antiques often found in old money families. A tile mosaic of the strange juxtaposition of an menorah and a cruxifix decorated the floor, emphasing the conflicting religious themes displayed. These pious images intermixed with others; animals engaged in battle and serpents winding around great merchant ships.

"This is my sanctuary, dear boy. I am honored to have you share it with me. Please – take a seat on my couch. I had Lycos of Athens make it mirror the ones in the imperial palaces I have heard so much about. You must have so many stories to tell about living among such fine things! I should like to hear a few of them to see how my humble home measures up to the houses of the nobility."

Crispus never heard of the designer Linus mentioned with a grand air as though Crispus should know him, but evidently Linus was all too ready to pay this man a large sum for shoddy work in Crispus' opinion. Linus's decorators were unschooled in the current Roman style of interior design, and it showed in what he called fine furniture. The garish creation was unlike any Crispus had seen in any domus, let alone an imperial palace. He struggled to find words that would not offend.

"Your decorators must know you well," he all he managed at last.

Smiling at the compliment, Linus clapped his hands, calling forth slave boys who appeared in the doorway, obedient as dogs. With a nod from Linus, they begin setting up a veritable feast on the center table. Roasted meats, pungent cheeses, bread, and rich stews appeared, but Crispus' spirits quelled at the sight. He had hoped for a brief meeting and then merciful sleep, but it seemed Linus had other plans for him. He ushered Crispus onto the couch and took up a position close beside him.

Linus accepted a cup of wine from his slaves and plucked a few grapes from one of the dishes laid before them. He looked around as though he was a spectator in his own house. "This villa has been in my family for generations, but no one ever thought to adorn it properly. My family thought it was audacious to display wealth, even in the house. Perhaps that is why I allow myself these vanities. I envied my friends' fine houses so when this villa fell to me, I sought to remedy that as soon as possible as a matter of principle."

"What principle is that?" Crispus asked, more out of boredom than anything else.

"The principle that money brings power and prestige, and that there are few with enough of it to keep their families safe for long," Linus said from around a mouthful of stewed beets. The juice dripped down his cheek and onto his robe, mixing like blood against the purple linen.

Crispus watched him with an almost morbid fascination. He had never encountered a man like Linus of Ephesus. As Linus greedily devoured his food, Crispus made a few small attempts to engage him and then realized there was no need, Linus was only talking to hear himself, so Crispus stopped listening early in his lecture. His thoughts wandered to Julia, then to Cassia. It was only when Linus began to speak of his own father that his words caught his attention and forged a common bond between them.

"My father is the reason my family is in Ephesus. My father converted at the urging of Aquila and Priscilla, the disciples who established the church here with Paul of Tarsus. Since then, my family has used our wealth to keep us safe. Now the burden has fallen to me, and I will not be the one to fail us. I too have a son and political aspirations for him that would benefit from the emperor's patronage."

"Have you not heard my father's edict against me? I can ask no favors from him. He wants me dead," Crispus said bitterly.

"A man seldom turns his back on his son forever. When you return to favor, a friendship between us will prove advantageous to both of us," he said, coming to it at last. Crispus was glad the wait was over. He knew the man wanted something from him. Charity was never a simple thing to men like Linus. "Allow me to assist you, and we will consider it a favor amongst new friends, eh?" Linus beamed at him with all the charm of a sewer rat.

The relief on Crispus' face was palatable. "*Uvas parati sunt ad messem*," he said.

Linus knit his brow. "I do not know that expression."

No surprises there, Crispus thought with just a touch of smugness born of his general distaste for Linus' pretentious nature. In Greek then, he repeated it for him. "The grapes are ready for harvest. It is an old saying my mother used, and it means you have come to the matter at last. I expected your hospitality would come at a price, Linus. Name it and let us put an end to these trifles. You may have it, whatever it is. I'm in no position to argue a point."

Crispus nestled deeper into the soft cushions behind him. He may as well be comfortable while listening to what he was sure would be an outlandish request.

Linus cleared his throat with a loud rumble. "Well, if I may confide in you, this war has greatly affected my fortunes. Since Diocletian's edicts seven years ago, I have depleted my resources, paying bribes to keep my family safe. I'm sure I don't need to explain to you how brutal these proscriptions have been for Christians. Your father of course has been loudest in denouncing them. Those in the west enjoy a safety that we wish for here. Your influence – when you are restored to him, of course – could mean an end to the drain on my purse and bring prosperity again to my doorstep." Here he stopped to take a healthy swig of his wine. "I'm tired of living in this constant state of fear and near poverty. Your earnest petition on my behalf is the price for the use of my home, and the care of that magnificent stallion my people retrieved for you. Refuse me, and I will not turn you out of doors tonight, but you must go in the morning. I would consider those actions unfriendly, and I do not house any except friends and family in my home."

Crispus listened patiently until that last remark. His face reddened without the help of the wine but he controlled his temper. "I have known many Christians in my life, of varying character and integrity, but none that would treat a guest this way. A petition to my father I can handle, threats I cannot, I will not." He rose to leave.

Linus rose as well, but in a panic. He clutched Crispus' arm; his red-rimmed eyes were more plaintive now. Desperation oozed from his pores like cheap oil through a sieve. He leaned towards Crispus until their faces were only inches apart. His breath washed over Crispus in a fetid wave.

"Please!" Linus cried. Gone was the carefree jokester of a few moments ago. In his place, a man who saw his last option slipping from grasp. "Please, my son was conscripted three years ago into Licinius

Augustus' army. He has managed to hide his Christian origins so far, but as this war drags on, I fear someone will expose him or he will expose himself out of guilt and become a martyr. With your father's help, I can see him home and safe again. You don't have to give your answer now, but think on it, I beg you. He has a wife and young son. Consider them. Please!" He released his vice-like grasp on Crispus' arm. They stood there together in silence until Linus cleared his throat finally when he realized Crispus intended to say nothing. "At any rate, you are safe in my house until morning. I promise you that."

Crispus doubted him. Linus was desperate, and desperate men often do the wrong things for reasons they think are right. Saving his son and finding the gold to keep his house afloat might prove too much temptation for Linus. Crispus wanted to follow his instincts, which sounded a warning to leave immediately, but the hour was late and without Viatoro he was stuck for the night. He did the best thing he could.

"Thank you Linus. If we could speak about it in the morning, I promise to give you the answer you seek." Linus could only offer grudging acceptance.

At daybreak, Crispus woke up in a clean and warm bed for the first time in weeks, and for that he was grateful. Once he gathered his wits, he noticed a teenaged girl standing just inside the doorway. In her hands, she carried a steaming bowl of wash water and a small towel. She presented it to Crispus with a submissive nod. "Dominus sent me to prepare you for the day and see to your needs. He awaits you in the triclinium."

Crispus breathed in the rose-scented steam

for several moments, clearing his head of the dreams of last night. He had dreamed of armies fighting and the stench of death on the field battles were over. He fought engagement after engagement in an endless cycle. Each one was the same – spears, swords and men screaming in pain while Crispus lost over and over again. The truth was, Linus was a peacock and a fool, but his concerns about his son were valid. Licinius was Crispus' uncle by marriage; he knew the man well. He resented Christians and put them on the front lines whenever he could. Perhaps it was mercy or perhaps just a longing to do something right after so long doing the wrong things, but Crispus decided to help Linus' son even if he could not trust the father.

"Does your dominus treat you well?" he asked the girl who waited for him to finish washing his face and hands. Small eyes blinked back at him, fearful but also intelligent. She knew the question he asked could mean her life.

"Please sir. It is not for me to say." Her voice was much older and experienced than her years.

"You needn't say at all. I can see the caution in your eyes. You are a good slave, but I am not asking you to betray your dominus. I just want to know more about him."

He moved closer to her as he spoke. His presence overpowered her. He knew she would tell him what he wanted to know. She shrunk away from him. It was enough to encourage Crispus. He pressed her further.

"What kind of man is your dominus, girl? Answer me. I promise I will not betray your confidence." Crispus smoothed back her hair, a few random strands that had fallen into her face. The simple gesture managed what his words could not and the girl broke her silence.

"The dominus was once kind to us, but since the young Quintus left for war, he has been different. Not cruel, not to me at least, he always favored me, but he calls me to his rooms less and less. There was a time when he prayed every day at the altar for his son, but he stopped about a year ago. Last night just before you arrived was the first time we have seen him pray that way. He said that he found a way to rescue Quintus and asked God to forgive him for what he was about to do."

Crispus did not need to hear any more. "Fetch writing materials" he told her. While she was gone, he dressed as quickly as possible. When she returned with a few scraps of vellum, a stylus, ink and sealing wax, he scratched out two short notes and pressed his signet ring into the hot wax. He handed them to the girl. One was to his aunt Constantina, Licinius' wife, and the other to his cousin Licinius II. In the letters, he asked them to locate Linus' son and send him home. It was a shallow gesture but hopefully enough to stop Linus from selling his hide to bounty hunters. The desperation in Linus last night told him he was not safe in the man's care no matter what promises he made.

"Give these to your dominus. Tell him I have no need of a second audience with him. My answer is yes, and you carry the promises he needs from me. In exchange, I require a fresh mount for my guard Donatus along with my horse's keep, and two months provisions from his household stores. Tell him I will be leaving within the hour."

The girl left to deliver his letters to Linus, and Crispus found his way to the stable to see if Viatoro was there as promised. When he reached it, he found Viatoro content, munching hay, his tail swatting at the flies that circled in the warm air of the stable. Relief flooded his heart at the sight of the familiar head bent low over a manger. In this unfamiliar place, nothing was more precious to him.

The stallion greeted him joyfully, nuzzling his face and neighing to him. "Viatoro...Viatoro," Crispus whispered while stroking his mane. Crispus paused a moment to look around him. Linus' stable was impressive. The animals were beautiful, well cared for, and Donatus would have a horse nearly as fine as Viatoro to ride. The animals were boisterous though, well aware of a stranger in their midst.

"Don't worry – we're as eager to leave as you are to see us gone." Crispus said aloud. "Where is Donatus, I wonder?" Crispus had not seen him since they arrived. "Donatus!" he shouted in case the giant was nearby.

"Sir?" Donatus popped up from a nearby stall. "I didn't hear you come in, but what I did hear were some troubling tales about Linus from the stable hands last night. I'm not sure we are safe here, after all."

"My thoughts exactly. Let us be gone from this place. I don't trust this man any further than I can see him!"

Before the morning was over, Crispus had said his farewells to Linus. The fat man was happy with what he clearly believed was his clever handling of an imperial son. As Crispus and Donatus stood near the entrance of the villa, a messenger bird with imperial markings took flight from the rear of the villa. The sight made Linus uncomfortable, and he shifted in his jeweled sandals. Crispus hoped desperately that it was not a sign of betrayal but something told him to be wary. He shrugged. There was nothing they could do about it now, except get far away from Ephesus. He and Donatus headed into the wilds of the Anatolian peninsula as fast as they could.

Chapter Five

Charietto

In another part of the world, in a dirty and ill-kept taberna, a solitary figure spotted his body slave across the room, a careworn Greek with a shuffling walk. Across the tables of loud gambling men and prostitutes, he watched the slave squinting into the darkness of the room to find him.

"Idiota! I'm over here!" shouted Charietto, the notorious and greatly feared bounty hunter. He came from lands east of the Rhine, where the people had no notion of submission, least of all to Rome. He raised his voice still louder over the din of clattering dice and curses. "Don't you know your dominus from these drunken fools and whores? Look here Adonis!"

Adonis still could not see or hear Charietto, but several others did and took exception at his words. They swung around, seeking the insolent owner of the voice. They found Charietto waiting; a storm that threatened to unleash his wrath on an unsuspecting world, or in this case, not so bright layabouts.

The bounty hunter sat hooded and cloaked in shadows, revealing little more than stained yellow teeth and thin, cruel lips. They stretched into a sneer that promised pain and plenty of it. Across his splayed legs, his left hand was coiled around a wickedly sharp blade. Those he offended cast sidelong looks at each other. Despite their bravado, no one wanted problems with a man like Charietto. The fervor died away to nothing save a few whispers and grumbled curses.

The old man spotted Charietto at last and hurried across the crowded room. He whispered frantically in his ear. "Dominus, you must meet the magistrate outside right now. General Pompeianus has sent a messenger for you."

"Message from Rome that finds me all the way here in Thessalonica? *Merde!* Well, he will have to wait 'til I'm done wettin' my throat. Tell 'em I'll be out when I've had my fill of wine…and *mammas et asini.*" He seized a passing barmaid who giggled in response. When she fell onto his lap, Charietto forgot any thoughts of Adonis or the men waiting for him outside the taberna.

Adonis persisted, much to Charietto's chagrin. He pleaded with his master. "Please, Dominus. He says it is a 'matter of the utmost gravity'. I think he means for you to come immediately. There may be consequences if you do not." The slave wrung his hands in misery.

With a frustrated sigh, Charietto pushed the girl from his lap. Standing to his feet, he towered a head above and was twice the size of any man present. "You best hope they aren't wastin' my time or I'll take my losses out of your hide!"

Adonis swallowed hard. "Yes Dominus, I know. They insisted they speak with you right away, or General Pompeianus would hear of it. I thought you would want to know."

Charietto took his time regardless, relishing the last drops of his wine before dropping a couple of coins on the table. He headed into the street where two men waited for him. One of them was a centurion by the looks of him while the other was a short, slender man dressed in the traditional toga of a magistrate. They motioned him to an alleyway behind the taberna.

The taller of the two, the centurion, had a Gallic look to him. He was red-haired with blue eyes and spoke in a broken, bastardized form of Greek. Charietto could hardly understand him. The man repeated himself several times before Charietto finally understood that his Excellency, General Pompeianus, wanted him to locate and kill Flavius Crispus, son of Constantine Augustus.

Madness! Charietto thought. Dread filled his heart. The entire world knew Constantine was at war with Maxentius, and now his best general wanted to kill Constantine's son. The man who did the deed for him might have a heavy price to pay one day if Constantine found it out.

Charietto chose his words carefully. He was on a slippery slope, and he could very well end up dead instead of Constantine's son. "Kill Flavius Crispus? For what, besides stupidity? His father has condemned him already. Why hire me to kill a man who is already dead in every way, except one?"

The tiny magistrate spoke up hastily. "Why is not your concern, just as how is not our concern. Just see to it. Your emperor commands it and will pay whatever you ask."

Charietto turned to him. "Never mind your price, this is my business," he replied sarcastically, "or you can find another man to do your dirty work for you. Even a fool knows not to trifle with Constantine. What if he changes his mind about his son? He may decide to kill the man reckless enough to do this thing, 'specially for his enemy and for a price."

The centurion leaned forward and spoke so only Charietto could hear him. "It is Emperor Maxentius himself who requests your services. On pain of death you must agree." His tone softened. "Trust me, friend. You don't want to know more. Do as we ask, and you will have more gold than you have ever seen in your life. You will be the richest man in the city!"

Charietto considered for a long moment, then gave his answer.

Chapter Six

Troubles in Nicomedia

Nicomedia. It was where all things began for Crispus. It was also where the bizarre happenings in his life led him to return. If 'returning' is what he could called fleeing for his life with dangerous men at his back. Strange the twist of fate that led him here, and stranger still the reality that Crispus would not enter the city as the conqueror he promised, but as an outsider forsaken by everyone who knew him. Almost everyone, he hoped. If there was anyone still on his side, they were here. Nicomedia was his sanctuary of last resort, the only place in the world he had a real chance to live beyond his pain and loss.

He had not been to Nicomedia since he was a young boy just beginning his teenage years, and much of it was different now. The city did not have the lightness and joy it held in his youth. The wars had reached them too, and the people were weary of sending their sons, fathers and husbands off to die to decide which despot would rule them.

Crispus passed beautiful libraries, basilicas, and other fine public works that emphasized the sophistication and dignity of the city's culture. A blur of images from his youth raced across his mind. Beside him, Donatus looked around in wonder, and even Viatoro began to bray excitedly at the spectacular before him.

"What place is this?" Donatus exclaimed. "I have been in many great cities but none as magnificent as this one. What extraordinary people you Romans are — you create the most remarkable places!"

A surge of pride swelled in Crispus' throat. "My father's people have been conquerors for a millennium, Donatus. I suppose they learned a few things along the way. They found this city a dying remnant and rebuilt it in its current glory." As they rode through the streets, Crispus noticed that Viatoro was beginning to attract too much of the wrong kind of attention. People pointed, whispered, and envy turned some of their stares hostile.

He pulled the stallion up short and dismounted. He knew well the figure he struck riding him. "It's no wonder they stare. I imagine it has been a long time since they have seen a Nisean on these streets. The last one was probably Viatoro's mother and that was many years ago. I don't suppose anyone recognizes me. My own family may not know me. I have been gone so long and changed so much."

"I hope for both our sakes they will be glad when they see you." Donatus offered.

"They will. My mother's blood is here. This is where I was born and reared, and this is where she died. My mother's family is from Armenia's royal house, but she and my Aunt Zenobia called Nicomedia home for many years. That's why we are here. My aunt won't turn me away, she loves me. Nicomedia is my best hope until my father comes to his senses, if he ever does."

"Time heals every wound. One day your father will remember you are the best part of him.

You'll see."

"I wish I had your optimism, but you don't know my father. He's can be as stubborn as a goat and twice as mean."

"You don't expect it to be a simple thing to regain his favor, do you? What they accuse you of is a terrible sin. To lay hands on..." Donatus did not finish. The withering look Crispus gave him stopped him. They walked along in an awkward silence, leading the horses behind them. The unfortunate reminder of why Crispus was in this predicament lay between them, a weighted stone best left alone.

Donatus kept close by Crispus' side as they ventured deeper into the city. They reached the heart of the forum where a play featuring Rome's politicians as buffoons delighted the gathered crowds. The actors poked fun at their betters, enjoying the whispers and laughs from the enraptured audience. They wore colorful costumes; yellows, daring oranges and blues swirled together in a cornucopia of sights and sounds to distract the people.

There was good reason to distract them. The tidings in Nicomedia had been dark for some time. Within the boundaries of the city, extreme poverty lived side by side with outrageous wealth, and the wealthy did not trouble to hide their good fortune. They displayed it for all to envy. Such disparity breeds unrest, and the city was perched on the edge of a blade. Open hostilities could not be far away.

Crispus had not been to the East in several years and was incredulous about the changes to his beloved city. Nothing was as it should be. It made him question the reception he might get once he reached his aunt's door. Zenobia's husband Boteiras had never cared very much for Crispus. Would he now turn him away from his door to avoid trouble? Would Zenobia allow it?

"It's been so long since I have seen my mother's sister. I wish I had better news for her. I doubt she will be surprised at my father's betrayal or Fausta's hand in it. She never liked Fausta. 'The Syrian she-wolf', she called her. Boteiras, I refuse to call the brute 'uncle' – had to force her to attend the wedding. No one could force my grandmother Helena though. She flat out refused to be present." He finished with a mirthless laugh.

"Your mother must have been held in high regard if even your father's mother took exception at him marrying another," Donatus said quietly.

Crispus looked away across the expanse of an agora they passed by. "She was – and my aunt is cut from the same cloth. Just with a sharper edge. Mother always said my rebellious nature came from her sister and that I was more connected to Zenobia's spirit than hers. I think she was right, and I've kept my revolutionary notions."

"One man's rebellion is another's freedom fight." Donatus said, swatting at a fly that was buzzing past him.

"More cryptic speech? Do you never tire of it, Donatus?" Crispus asked him with a smirk.

He slapped the giant man on the back, and they shared a rare, lighthearted moment of friendship. It helped Crispus relax before he reached his aunt's residence which was on the edge of town. Zenobia and Boteiras shared a large estate that belonged to Minervina while she lived. It was where Crispus had taken his first steps and where Viatoro was born.

Crispus tried to plan what he would say to Zenobia when he saw her – she would surely ask him what happened with his father. He did not yet know if he could bear for her to know the truth. His only option was to lie to her, something he had never been good at doing. The last thing he wanted was to fall short in her eyes, so like his mother's. To see disapproval in them would crush the little spirit he had left.

"I am not a praying man, Donatus, but you are. Petition your god for me, that my aunt takes us in and that she does not ask me too many questions. I don't think I can survive seeing her heartbroken over my misdeeds. It would be like disappointing my mother. I know I was wrong, but everyone should have a second chance. I think I deserve one, too."

"Domina, there are men at the door who claim to be your nephew Crispus and his guard. They ask to speak to you." The doorkeeper came closer to whisper in Zenobia's ear. "They seek sanctuary." He bowed his head, awaiting her instructions. Everyone in the household knew about Constantine's edict and that it was only a matter of time before the boy showed up at Zenobia's door.

"Crispus? You may raise your face to me, Erastos, and tell me why on earth you have left my nephew outside my door as a common stranger? See him in at once!"

"But Domina, the edict – Dominus gave orders…" The man's voice trailed off as Zenobia silenced him with a raised brow. Zenobia was a singularly beautiful woman, striking features, long-limbed and slender, like most beautiful women, even the sight of her angry was a pretty one.

"Are you questioning me, Erastos? I don't care what my husband says about it. My sister's ashes rest within these walls. I will not deny her only child refuge. See them to the Triclinium and have food prepared. I will inform my husband of his arrival myself!" She left the room in a whirl of pale yellow, a sunray in motion. Her stola flared out behind her and her sandals tapped a rapid beat across the floor mosaics in her haste.

Zenobia found Boteiras and his most trusted slave, Abercius, sequestered in his tablinum. Boteiras was taller than his wife and nearly as thin. His had a pinched, fox-like face but his manner was more weasel than anything else, stingy and greedy.

Lavender oil burned heavy in the room, giving the air a peace-inducing scent and the only sound came from pebbles sliding across an abacus as Boteiras counted his mounting debts against his income with a worried frown. The two men were so intent on their task that neither of them noticed that Zenobia had joined them.

Boteiras was in the midst of stretching and rubbing his neck as though Atlas himself had burdened him, when he glanced up to see his wife standing in front of the curtains lining his doorway. The curtains engulfed her tiny frame as she pulled them together behind her. Boteiras had given her strict orders against intrusion. The annoyance on his face did not help matters. Zenobia hesitated before giving him the news that her out-of-favor nephew had landed at their doorstep. His reaction was not unexpected.

"Your sister's bastard appears at the door, a harbinger raven, and yet you stand delivering the news as a gift rather than a curse upon us. Send him away!" Boteiras planted white-knuckled fists on his desk and rose to his feet, trembling with anger.

Zenobia raised a hand to stop him. She stood as solid as the granite-topped desk between them. "We cannot turn him away, Boteiras! The same blood that flows in my veins flows in his. I never betrayed Minervina in life, and I won't do it now in death." After a short pause, she thought to add "…my love."

Boteiras was unappeased. "But why does he come here and foist his miseries upon us? Does he think we are unaware aiding him is treason? We'll be nailed to crosses beside him!" He ran a hand angrily through his thick mass of dark curls, already in disarray.

"That will never happen. This was his mother's house, how can we possibly refuse? Her ghost will come back to haunt us both! Come, he's waiting in the triclinium for us." Zenobia came close. She affectionately stroked his cheek.

Boteiras was not in the mood for her charms. "I'm not finished, Zeni," he said. He slid away from her caress, but he was softening to her, that much was clear. "My cooperation comes with conditions. I won't forbid him, but neither will I welcome him until I send word to Constantine. I will not have our lives in danger for your dead sister's child. I must have his consent. And on your part, you must promise to abide without complaint, whatever the emperor decides. Is that understood?"

Zenobia had no intention of leaving Crispus to his fate, but there was no need to go into that now. She nodded gratefully. "Thank you, husband. Shall we go to him then?" she asked as she took his hand in hers.

Zenobia and Boteiras headed to the triclinium where they found Crispus on a couch devouring an assortment of delicacies as though he had not eaten for a month. Behind him, Donatus munched on an apple, crunching so loudly Zenobia was offended. She had no idea who the massive stranger behind her nephew might be, but clearly he had no manners. Donatus watched Zenobia and Boteiras enter the room with a suspicious eye. He remained in his place standing behind Crispus, waiting to be dismissed.

Crispus nodded in his direction. "Donatus, you have waited long enough to fill your belly. There is no danger for me here. You may go."

Zenobia spoke to a servant girl, "Have meat and bread put out for him, and a good wine." She said to Donatus with a smile and an attempt at charm. It went unheeded.

"Thank you madam," Donatus said in a careful voice before following a servant from the room. He continued to eye his hosts, so much so that Zenobia was offended again, though her husband seemed oblivious to the insult of Donatus' intense stare.

"How ever did you come by such a creature? He looks ready to carve us into pieces on the spot. Does he not know you are among family here?" Zenobia exclaimed after he left them.

"I met him on the ship from Ariminum. He served with my grandfather, and now he serves me at a time when my friends are few."

Boteiras' voice dripped with contempt. "On that at least you speak the truth. I wonder what tales you will spin for us about the reasons for your death decree? No doubt there is some excuse or blame to lay at someone else's feet! Do you understand the peril you place on this house boy? Your situation is precarious, and you have appeared from nowhere to visit your troubles on your aunt! Do you care nothing for her well-being? What if your father has us executed for harboring you?"

Refusing to be baited, Crispus gave no answer. He stared back with as much pride as he could muster. Boteiras moved closer. He placed himself within inches of Crispus' face.

"Do you hear me speaking to you, you impertinent child? You call yourself a soldier, yet you know nothing of the world and are little more than a suckling babe! Shedding the blood of peasants made you bold enough to lay hands on your father's wife, and now you flee like a child to hide behind Zenobia's skirts!" Boteiras puffed out his chest. "And I shall do as I have always done, I will snatch you from behind them to face your justice! I intend to send word to your father that Zenobia wants to provide you sanctuary. You had better hope the esteem he holds for this family will give him a reason to show you mercy."

Crispus wanted to remain silent, but his uncle's arrogance infuriated him. "Esteemed? I didn't know that applied to you, Boteiras. If I remember correctly, this house belonged to my mother's family long before you came here. I am always welcome in it."

Boteiras' face turned from its usual red to deep purple. He clutched at his robes as though he wished they were Crispus' neck. "How dare you! I am the master of this house! If it were not for your aunt's misguided affection, I would turn you out of it immediately. Say another word to me, and I will, regardless of her pleas!"

His eyes bulged in his head, and his face twitched in a way that was unsettling to watch. Crispus remained calm during his outburst. He looked to Zenobia to intervene. She did not disappoint. She rushed to his defense as she did when he was a child caught in wrongdoing.

"Calm yourself, husband. The boy has only just arrived and no doubt weariness and worry color his words. I'm sure he will tell us what happened in Mediolanum in due course. For now, let him rest." She stepped forward to squeeze Crispus' hand and kiss his cheek. She looked back at her husband; her eyes beseeched him to hold his peace. And thankfully he did.

"I have been riding for days. Thank you, Aunt Zenobia." He turned to Boteiras. "Uncle, you do not know the facts. I am innocent, but I lay my fate at your feet. Inform on me to my father if it pleases you. I would expect nothing less."

"I'll do it first thing in the morning, and I hope he sends orders to have you scourged and crucified! I'll gladly do the honors myself! Zenobia, I'm going back to my work – do not disturb me again!" Boteiras stormed from the room.

Zenobia turned to Crispus. She graced him with a wan smile and cupped his face in her hands. "Well, that went better than expected, I suppose.

Years have passed, and yet it is as though you are a child again seeking protection for some misdeed. You may give me the details later, but for now I must know, did you do this thing they claim?"

Crispus looked into her eyes. Though he wanted to tell her the truth, he could not admit his part in his downfall. The lie fell easier from his tongue than he would have thought possible. "Aunt, I have done some things I am ashamed to speak of, but laying violent hands on Fausta is not one of them. She is a —"

Zenobia cut him off. "Enough. I have heard what I needed. Say no more. We shall pray that the coming weeks bring good news and that you may remain here, safe from your father and his Praetorians. Get some rest, my boy. You are safe in this house. Adelpha will see to your comfort. Welcome back, your mother would be pleased you found your way to me."

Crispus headed off down the hallway with his aunt's maid, too happy for words. He stopped for a moment to look around him and breathe deep of the familiar scents he did not know he missed until he smelled them again.

"I'm home. At last, I'm home." And he knew he would sleep well that night.

The days in Nicomedia under his aunt and uncle's roof passed quickly and uneventfully save for Boteiras being as unpleasant as possible. Before the moon finished one cycle, the news they had all been anticipating arrived at last.

It came one warm evening right after the garden flowers had begun to bloom in the peristyle. It was where the family spent much of their time. They had been enjoying a quiet meal; no one else was there except Crispus, his aunt and uncle, and Donatus, who stood in the far corner, as he always did whenever Boteiras was around.

The doorkeeper arrived with the message that an imperial courier waited in the vestibule. Boteiras stopped chewing his pork loin long enough to issue orders for the courier to come to them. He flashed Crispus a scathing look of triumph and rubbed his hands together. Crispus pretended he was unconcerned, but his heart beat painfully in his chest, and suddenly he could not breathe. He drank deep of his wine to steady himself. He nearly spewed it from his mouth when he risked an upward glance at the courier.

The man walking towards him was none other than his cousin, Licinius. Crispus could not speak. His face spread into a wide smile, and he ran forward to meet him. He grasped Licinius and squeezed him in a enveloping hug. Finally, Crispus broke away to face him.

"If you are here as a messenger, cousin, I fear the report you carry. He hasn't sent you as a final mercy to a condemned man, has he?" Crispus searched Licinius' face for some clue. Licinius gave none. Instead, he motioned to a guard standing behind him. The soldier passed him a small roll of wax-sealed vellum. He held it so that the seal was visible.

"The seal of Constantine Augustus. Witness his edict regarding the renegade soldier Flavius Valerius Crispus," Licinius intoned in halting formal Latin.

At hearing himself called a renegade, Crispus

stiffened. On cue, Licinius looked up from his recitation. He smiled at his cousin to calm him.

"Citizens of the Empire, thus proclaims your emperor – Flavius Crispus Valerius Constantinus, called Crispus is hereby banished to the city of Nicomedia on pain of death should he be found outside of it. He is stripped of all rank, command and favor of the emperor."–

Here, Crispus' sharp breath disrupted the reading. Zenobia quieted him with a single raised finger to her lips.

Licinius went on. "He shall suffer under *Damnatio Memoriae* from this day forward and his name shall not be spoken or written. By the hand of Constantine Augustus, a reward of 100,000 sestertii will be provided to the citizen who, upon finding Crispus outside Nicomedia, captures him and provides him to the magistrate for summary execution."

No one spoke, not even Licinius as he rerolled the document. The full implications of the emperor's decision hung unspoken in the air around them until Boteiras, with a joyful whoop of laughter, gave them a voice.

"A general no more and stripped of your honorable name? Dignity shattered like a broken piss pot and a punishment fitting your arrogance!" His satisfaction was boundless.

Zenobia did her best to help. She cried out in happiness, "You may remain at my side, as your mother would wish! What joyful news Licinius brings us!"

Licinius agreed, nodding, "He does not decree death – anything short of that is a victory." Seeing

Crispus' face in anguish, he added, "In a manner of speaking."

Crispus could do nothing more than stare miserably at all of them. So many emotions flooded his body he had trouble standing. He collapsed into his chair. Once again, his father blessed him in one breath and cursed him with the next. "He may as well have killed me," he muttered. "How will I reclaim my honor without men to wage their swords alongside mine? When I left Treverorum, I did not believe it would be for the last time. It is impossible to consider!"

"Nephew, your father allows you to remain here, safe and alive. What more can you ask of the fates, and what did you expect?" Zenobia was genuinely puzzled by his reaction.

Ever patient with his aunt, Crispus turned to her to explain the true meaning of the decree. "No calling for my death is a relief of course, but he has done me no favors here. Since I first joined him in battle, my father has groomed me to command, to strive to return Rome to her past glories. The men are like family to me, the life blood running in my veins, as strong as his blood within me! No, this cannot stand!"

Zenobia gazed at him in amazement. She hardly knew where to begin. "My dear boy, you are your father's son, a noble calling, but you also belong to your mother. She allowed no person or deed to reduce her to something she was not; she kept her dignity and the pride until death. Your mistakes do not define you unless you allow them. Show your father that your life is your own, not his to give or take from you. You didn't come here to die, but to live! And you shall not hide behind the walls of this villa. To the contrary, let it serve as your rostra, a platform to reach the people and set an example of redemption and grace sorely needed in this city. Nicomedia can be the place where your life begins again with fresh purpose and focus."

Boteiras noticed an idea hatching in her words. "What are you proposing? It cannot be anything to our benefit."

Zenobia's face was a mask of innocence. She dismissed Boteiras' concerns. "Nothing. Well, I'm merely making an observation that since the decree allows Crispus to remain in the city, he should know its people. I was thinking that a feast day would be a good way to reintroduce himself. And besides, who doesn't like a good party? It has been some time since we had one and here's a good reason."

The suggestion piqued Licinius' interest. "Excellent idea. A party! Let's celebrate Crispus' reentry into Bithynian society!"

Crispus was the only one who had not spoken up about the plan. He was quiet, contemplating it. "There are people here I desperately would like to know again, perhaps a party is indeed the best way to start out here. Of course, I accept. You honor me Aunt Zenobia, I'm eternally grateful to you," he added as a deliberate afterthought, "and to Boteiras as well."

Boteiras showed him what he thought of his gratitude with a loud, derisive snort.

Zenobia shot him an annoyed look but otherwise ignored him, as did the others. To Crispus and Licinius she exclaimed, "All the best people will be invited to celebrate one of Nicomedia's favorite sons! Who would not turn out to see the fallen prince, now reborn as an honored denizen of the city?" Zenobia was growing excited about the prospect of planning an extravaganza.

In contrast, her husband maintained his dour expression. "And no doubt drag us into poverty to pay for it," he muttered under his breath. Zenobia heard him, but again did not bother with a reply. She turned her back, swung her hair, and clasped arms with both Crispus and Licinius. The trio walked away to plan a feast to shame all others.

Boteiras watched them walk away. "Zenobia is a sentimental fool. She will throw everything away for her sister's unworthy bastard. Well, we shall see about that, I have another idea for what to do about Crispus!"

Bad news travels fast, and in a seedy brothel, in Thessaly this time, Charietto the hunter was slowly unrolling a scroll. His lack of enthusiasm and fumbling movements revealed his frustration. For weeks, he had chased unreliable rumors of Constantine's son from one far-flung location to another, all without success. His men soon tired of the game. They would have deserted him already if not for their fear of him and their need for money. But now, Charietto's fists closed excitedly around the scrap of vellum. As he read it, a queer, sinister smile played about his lips. He cleared his throat to shout for attention. The men around him left their grinning whores, and the ones throwing dice paused in their game. All eyes were on Charietto.

"Word comes from Rome; the boy Crispus has been spotted. He's in Nicomedia, and this time the information is reliable. His uncle there gave him up. He's in exile there and won't expect an ambush. It's almost too easy!" He laughed aloud and slapped his hands against the table, tumbling the dice to the floor.

Charietto pulled a careworn map from the small satchel he carried with him. With one hand, he swept the table free of remaining clutter, including the gambling stakes of gold and silver coins. There was a mad scramble on the floor as the women leaped to grab them. A lucky few managed to get one or two; the rest got only slaps and curses for their trouble.

Charietto laid the map down for all to see while he plotted a course to Nicomedia. The map was covered in large red dots of hardened wax, each denoting a kill he made over the years. Charietto traced his finger along a line to Nicomedia. There were no red dots covering it yet.

Charietto chuckled. "A chance to add my blood mark to a new place. We make for Nicomedia!

Chapter Seven

A Feast to Shame All Others

The happenings in Nicomedia excited more than Charietto and his minions. All the best people, the most respected tongues in the land, were wagging about the roguish young high nobleman under exile in their city. Teenaged girls swooned in their bedchambers, their mothers plotted to get close to him and the fathers and husbands plotted how to keep him as far away from their womenfolk as possible.

The emperor's son or not, he was banished and in disgrace. The question on every tongue was why and the speculations ran rampant. His father banished him for thievery, something precious to him, no doubt – no, he ran away from his father because he did not want to fight anymore – "Fools!" those who claimed to know for sure cried out. He stole his father's best horse, didn't they know? They swore to the heavens and Hades too that they alone knew the truth. Nobody got it right, but everyone joined in the fun of guessing, and the speculation was endless. Crispus knew it would reach Julia's ear soon enough. She had to know he was in the city. He thought she would have visited him by now, but perhaps the sting of their parting words still lingered in her mind.

The notion upset Crispus more than he cared to admit. The only remedy was to swallow his pride and reach out to her first. After a hard-fought debate with himself and with Licinius making snide little jokes as he prepared it, he sent a messenger with a formal invitation for her family to join him at his celebration. That he should have to make the first move irritated him, but he understood why. *I should have written sooner,* he thought. An unexpected stab of guilt and regret struck a sour note in his chest. *What if she says no?*

When the invitation arrived by courier, it threw Emperor Galerius' household into chaos like every other family who received one. This event was special, starting with the invitation. It was delivered by a gold-painted courier dressed as Mercury in a winged hat, pointed-toe boots and little more than a twist of fabric at his waist. The invitation itself was hidden inside a tiny box he presented to Julia's mother, the Empress Galeria. It was almost indecent, but Galeria was enchanted with the pageantry nonetheless. Julia was less impressed with the messenger than with the sealed box. She waited anxiously while her mother enjoyed the moment and took her time opening it.

Galeria was forever the debutante, seen at every event with or without her husband, but always with Julia tucked at her side like another of her jewels. Julia sighed deeply watching her mother. It was as though opening an invitation, no matter how exciting, was the highlight of her month and the sad fact is, it probably was. Julia could not bear the thought she might share a similar fate.

Galeria opened the box with excited, fumbling hands. "Flavius Crispus. That's who this is for? What a joke! I heard that Zenobia, that silly woman, was planning a symposium for him, but this is too much!"

Julia seized the gold-etched vellum from her mother and sat down to read, still in shock. "Crispus sent this to me? I knew he was in the city, but I've heard nothing from him. Now this?" Her golden-brown eyes darkened to the color of bronze in her anger. Crispus had some nerve sending her an invitation like any random girl on his list. Her maids rushed to her side while her mother sent the courier away then came to sit down beside her.

"What is wrong with you, girl? This is wonderful news! Zenobia plans to premier her disgraced nephew at a party, pretending all is well? The gossip will go on for weeks…months, I'm sure of it!" Galeria was beside herself with glee.

Julia did not move. She was not sure how to feel about any of it. Part of her was excited, but the rest of her was angry, nervous and anxious. "So his thoughts turn to me now, after weeks? Not a word when it would have mattered, but now he invites me because it's safe for him to entertain? I won't go, mother. I simply won't go!"

"Of course you're going, you silly girl. We are both going!" Galeria reached into the box again where there was another scrap of vellum. Glancing quickly at the name on the outside of it, she pressed it into Julia's hands. "He sent the invitation along with a personal message for you. Read it. Perhaps it's good news! You father's health grows more fragile by the day. Soon, we will need protection from his enemies. This is not a game, child. You scorn my social appearances, but they may save our lives one day."

"Water," Julia muttered to her maids. She was so agitated, her throat threatened to close. One of the servants rushed away, returning with water and a fan. As Julia gulped loudly and the girl fanned her, her mother rose to stand over her with an angry scowl and hands that seemed ready to snatch the vellum she just handed to Julia.

She adjusted the gold bracelets encircling her arms as her irritation with Julia grew. "If you are quite finished with the theatrics my dear, read his message. And of course, you will entertain his attentions. He is an imperial son. I insist upon it!"

"You sell me too cheap, mother. Crispus can do nothing for us. He's in exile, or did you forget?" She jumped up from her couch, spilling water down the front of her stola. A handmaiden rushed forward with a towel.

Galeria did not say a word. She walked past her drenched daughter with a chuckle and sat on the couch. She patted the space next to her.

"Sit," she commanded in a voice not to be disobeyed. She began patiently, "Listen to me, my dove, we cannot afford to turn away suitors, no matter how unlikely. Given the stakes, we must consider everyone of note, including Constantine's son."

Julia took the towel offered by her maid. She dabbed at her stola impatiently then sat down beside her mother in a huff. Her mood toward anything from Crispus was not improved by sitting cold and wet, trying to listen to it.

Galeria picked up the discarded note and read aloud. "*My dearest Julia,*" it began.

Julia made a scoffing sound in her throat. "He begins all wrong!"

"Shh, how should he address you? Wife? Lover? You are neither...yet," warned Galeria. She read on:

"*I pray this letter finds you in good health. I hope you will forgive my delay, but I was unable to find the words to write to you sooner. I know our last meeting was less than happy, but I remain hopeful that you will find it in your heart to put aside your feelings and lend your support to a friend. To that end, I ask you to attend the celebration my dear Aunt Zenobia is planning for me. I shall count it joy itself to see you by my side. I should also like to discuss how we may rekindle our friendship which has suffered as a casualty of this terrible war.*

My fidelity always,
Flavius Valerius Crispus."

Galeria dropped the note onto Julia's lap. "Well, there he is, on his hands and knees practically, begging you for an audience. How can you refuse his pleas when he is so sincere?"

Julia was noncommittal. "That remains to be seen. If you insist that I go, then I will, but do not expect me to shed tears of joy at the prospect. I detest him, I truly do and I'm going to refuse him, on principle even if I attend."

Her mother indulged her with a slight smile. "Fine, if that makes you feel better about it but I think you are too excited for your protests to be real. I recall your fondness for the boy. You have not even managed to convince me your feelings for him are dead, so you can hardly expect to persuade him!"

With that Galeria left and Julia was on her own to sort out her emotions about Crispus.

"I'm a fool if I allow him back into my life. What can I do? I care for him still, but I would die rather than have him know it!"

But even as she spoke the hateful words aloud, she knew she did not mean them.

The day of the celebration came with a flurry of activity in the household of Zenobia and Boteiras. Slaves busied about, scrubbing the floors to a brilliant shine, replacing the curtains with newly-woven ones, stringing decorations and bringing in exotic plants and trees. Intoxicating scents wafted from the rear of the house as the chef and kitchen staff worked feverishly to prepare a glorious feast worth remembering.

Zenobia raised her voice above the din, ordering yet another change to the menu. "Adelpha, I want the roasted peacock served after the fish, not before it. The peacock is too heavy on the palate, and I don't want any more of that disgusting chicory sauce; use the garum instead."

Adelpha, Zenobia's body slave, issued orders to the other servants as quickly as her domina gave them to her. She trailed behind Zenobia closer than her shadow, doing her best to anticipate the whims of her mistress.

Crispus and his uncle endured a rare morning meal together in her absence. For Zenobia's sake, Crispus chanced a polite greeting, but when met with a surly grunt from Boteiras in between bites of food, he gave up the charade of comradery altogether.

Boteiras and Crispus ate in stony silence, awkward and uncomfortable but for the arrival of Licinius at the table. "Crispus... Boteiras – basking in each other's company again, I see. How you two manage to live under the same roof together is a wonder to me, but it's helpful this morning. Crispus, I was hoping to catch you alone while Zenobia is occupied with her preparations, and here I find you entertaining this old coot!" He slapped Boteiras on the back as he spoke, causing the man to swallow a large mouthful of boiled egg before he was ready.

Boteiras sputtered while a slave whacked his back and passed him his wine cup. When he regained control of himself, he was livid. "Licinius, you ass! You nearly choked me. I loathe the pair of you. The sooner you are away from these walls, the better!" He lurched to his feet.

Licinius leaned against the base of a large bust of Marcus Aurelius. With his arms crossed, he eyed Boteiras in mock wonder. "The paterfamilias begging his honored guests to leave? Where are your manners, Boteiras?

Boteiras gaped red-faced at Licinius. His lips worked furiously to find curses, but he only succeeded in looking more foolish than ever.

Licinius took the opportunity to add insult to injury. "Shh, old man, think before you speak. Don't embarrass yourself. Crispus may be out of favor, but

I'm not. One word from my lips will see your throat slit and those slave boys you chase around will have some relief from you." He made a crude gesture with his hand and mouth to torment the man. While Boteiras boiled like a pot over the fire, Licinius laughed and grabbed Crispus. Together they beat a hasty retreat leaving Boteiras alone and enraged. They headed towards the exercise yards behind the villa where they could be certain Boteiras would never follow them.

The palaestra[10] was a place they could be sure Boteiras would not venture. Once there, Crispus allowed a touch of impatience to show. "What is so important that you must drag me out here? I'm happy to dodge Boteiras, but I don't have a mind for sport today. Julia will be here with her parents by nightfall." With her arrival so close at hand, he found it difficult to concentrate on anything else.

"So? What of it? Many people will be here by nightfall. It is a party, after all. I didn't know she moved you so. Have you been pining away for Julia when you should have been killing barbarians? Surely not!" Licinius joked in mock surprise.

"Are you never serious? I have not been pining for her!"

"Well, that remains to be seen. Julia may be here tonight, but that doesn't matter, does it? In a few days you will be riding with your men, striking fear in the hearts of your enemies and amassing glory." Licinius spoke casually but his last sentence caught Crispus off guard and it showed.

---

[10] Exercise yard, borrowed from Greek name for outdoor wrestling school. Enclosed area usually adjacent to the baths.

"What are you saying?" Crispus looked thoroughly confused. The rumors around the villa were that Licinius must have come to Nicomedia to do more than deliver a message. Now Crispus would hear the rest of the story.

"Your father did not select me for this trip, I volunteered. I begged him to allow me to deliver his decision to you, not because I thought you needed my help, but because I need yours. Return to Treverorum with me. Your men await you. All of them are ready to desert their new generals and return to your side."

Crispus was shocked. "You turn against my father?"

"On the contrary, I serve him and you. The witch Fausta has blinded him to the truth, but one day he will awaken from her spell. Until then, there is plenty we can do. I want to organize a raiding party that can terrorize the enemy supply lines. It will enrich us and also help your father's cause, which is your cause too."

"Are you sure you want to risk your life for me again?" Crispus asked, only partly in jest.

Licinius grinned. "What else is there for me to do with it?"

"Well, you might want to reconsider; I'm a man without family ties now. The men may not follow me."

"Your men are loyal and always devoted to you. They will follow you anywhere! Just think of the blow we will strike for Rome! Join me Crispus, and we will rain terror on our enemies in ways they cannot imagine."

Before Crispus could answer him, a serving girl appeared at his side. "The domina summons you, sir. Another messenger has arrived for you."

Crispus was glad for the interruption. "Come, Aunt Zenobia is waiting for us but the answer is no. The last thing I want to do is lead a clutch of raiders. We can be of more use to the war effort other ways. Right now, it doesn't seem that way, but we can, of that I am sure."

Exasperated but unable to object, Licinius reluctantly followed Crispus back inside to find Zenobia.

Along the way, he speculated on who Crispus' messenger could be this time. "I'll lay coin it's another private message from some love-struck society wench. I'm not sure which is the bigger draw, you or me, but I intend to take full advantage of it. Some lucky girl is going to leave this house without her virtue intact tonight!"

Crispus joined him in a hearty laugh. "You never change. Are women and war all you care about?"

Licinius replied with his personal truth. "What else is there?"

Crispus just shook his head. He clapped his cousin on the back and mussed his hair. Inside the villa, they found Zenobia waiting for them in the atrium, message in hand.

"What is it?" Crispus said, rushing to her side. She held out the note to him. Crispus read it in silence. In a neat hand he recognized instantly as belonging to Julia, there it was, her dismissal:

To Crispus, son of Constantine. I regret I cannot attend, having more pressing business at home.

Yours sincerely,
Julia Galeria Valerius

Crispus was stunned. With her short note, Julia reminded him of his place, defined their relationship and rebuked his peace offering in one stroke. If it were not in Julia's hand, he would not have believed she wrote the thing.

"She's not coming" he said, stating the obvious. He passed the note to Zenobia who had no response as she read the contents. She moved to comfort him but he walked past her in a daze. All week he had been anticipating his first sight of Julia, and now it was not going to happen. Needle-sharp frustration pricked his heart. The pain of it caused him to flinch as though he was not a battle-hardened commander but a heartsick child. That Julia should have this power over him was a strange sensation and he did not like it.

"Damn her!" he muttered angrily. He threw up his hands before stalking off into the recesses of the house.

Licinius went to follow him, but a warning glance from Zenobia stopped him. "Leave him alone for a while. The hearts of women are fickle. It's better he finds out now. Some of us are not so quick to forgive the men that hurt us, regardless of the reason."

"You wounded plenty in your day, Zenobia, so I suppose you would know." Licinius was only half-joking, but obeyed her and did not follow his cousin.

Crispus found his way to the stables, as he

always did when he was very troubled. He made light conversation with the stable hands and spent time with Viatoro, brushing his mane until the strands gleamed as bright as the noonday sun. He did not reappear until late in the afternoon shortly before the first guests were due to arrive. He scarcely had time to bathe and dress but he felt better as he went about his party preparations.

Zenobia began to think he intended to hide away from Julia and not attend his own celebration, when Crispus finally appeared. He stood before her in the atrium immaculately dressed in a toga of fine black wool. Underneath it, his tunic was a rich emerald green color and shimmering. His face was freshly shaved, his hair scented with myrrh and his nails expertly manicured. Crispus shined like new-minted gold.

"Well, what do you think?" He turned slowly for her inspection. The green of the tunic caught the hazel in his eyes, producing a striking effect. He had taken care with his clothing; he wanted to look his absolute best in case Julia decided to attend after all. He confided to Zenobia, "I thought to wear my armor, but it will remind the guests of what I have lost, rather than what I have gained. I thought this a better choice."

Zenobia agreed. "You'll have to fight off the ladies, and they will be fighting each other over you all night." She clapped her hands excitedly. "This party will be on everyone's lips for months, years even. Our family will be the envy of the whole city!"

"As you say, but the only face I want to see tonight has refused the invitation. I wonder who else will decide to stay away to snub me as Julia did?"

Crispus could not help grousing a little despite the festive mood in the house.

"Still rankled over Galerius' daughter? Be patient. There will come another opportunity to woo her." Zenobia stroked his cheek. "Cheer up, my boy. Julia is not the only girl in Nicomedia. There will be plenty of others to occupy you tonight. I sent invitations to everyone of note – there's bound to be someone else who captures your interest."

"Perhaps Aunt Zenobia, but you're wrong about Julia. I'm not bothered in the least by her absence. When she hears of this night and the fun she missed, she will be the one who's sorry, not me."

"The first guests arrive!" The doorkeeper shouted the news. Outside there was the noise of rising female voices. "Adelpha, summon the party staff! Oh, and where is my husband, and Licinius for that matter? I have not seen either of them for hours."

"I think Boteiras is hiding away in his rooms, but Licinius will turn up sooner or later. He wouldn't miss this for anything." Crispus and Zenobia went to the vestibule together to offer welcome greetings as the doorkeeper admitted several well-dressed ladies into the house. Once the tide of guests started, it went on for the better part of an hour as everyone trying to be fashionably late, arrived at the same time.

The men clustered together while the women milled about, mostly in pairs, each a dazzling specimen of Roman womanhood. Their milk and honey-bathed skin shone in all the radiant shades of the human rainbow from alabaster to obsidian. The ladies all had intricately styled hair in browns, reds, sun-streaked blondes and striking black. They were draped in jewels; wearing pearls, opals, rubies, and emeralds. The women were all different, yet somehow all the same.

They bored Crispus on sight. He ignored their expectant expressions as he kissed cheeks and walked around greeting guests. Zenobia led everyone into the atrium where the entertainers she hired for the night assembled to start their performace. The dancers climbed and tumbled over each other while a trio of lively harpists in flowing stolas sat plucking away with flute players and a cymbalist to accompany them.

As the ladies moved past him in clouds of perfume and twittering laughter, Crispus sighed deeply. "Well, I don't know why I expected to see anything other than a gaggle of cackling geese. These vapid creatures are better suited to Licinius," he said aloud, as he turned away from the party to find a quiet place to drink himself into a stupor.

From behind him, a dulcet voice filled his ears, mocking him with gentle laughter. "And who is suited to you Crispus? Have your appetites changed since I last saw you, and you no longer enjoy the company of women?"

Crispus turned as slowly as he could force himself, knowing who spoke to him by the thrill running up his spine.

She stood in the doorway, clothed in a simple blue stola more suited for an afternoon visit than a formal party, but Julia Galeria was more beautiful in it than any woman he had ever seen. His lingering gaze traveled from her tiny gold and sapphire-trimmed sandals to the crown of her head where a small diadem rested amid the flowing brown waves of her hair. She was a rare gem, unaffected by the hand of any man and simply stunning to him. Caught unawares by the strength of his emotions, Crispus resisted the urge to take her into his arms on the spot.

"Julia." The hoarse way he whispered her name embarrassed him. He quickly cleared his throat and tried again. "Julia. Good of you to come, my dear." That was better, he hoped.

He did not fool her. "You look like you see my ghost instead of my face. Surprised that I'm here, I suppose?"

She smiled the same crooked grin that was hers as a child, but the little girl in her was long gone. On the day he rejected her, she had been too young and naïve for him, but he wondered how he could have missed the blossoming woman that must have been under the surface, even then. As Crispus lowered his head to kiss her cheek, Julia's careful façade cracked in spectacular fashion, revealing her true heart. Her cheeks warmed to the color of ripe cherries, her breathing quickened, and an unbidden smile broke across her face like morning sunshine.

She was enchanting and Crispus reveled in her beauty. He paused just before his lips met her skin. Julia froze, not wanting to meet his eye, but she was drawn to him nevertheless. Crispus returned her smile with one of his own. He brushed his lips across her cheek, and as he made to pull away, he rested them for the briefest moment against the corner of her mouth.

Crispus had known war since he was seventeen, had killed men and dodged knives long enough to recognize the excitement that now raced through his veins like wine drunk too fast. Bolts of energy ran the length of his body, invigorating him in the white-hot space between life and death where true bravery makes its home. Now, at this moment with Julia, it was as if he was drawing a final breath before dying happy.

Julia looked into his eyes, and the years and bitterness melted away. The hardness left her face, replaced with joy. "Crispus, you haven't changed one bit!" she giggled, pushing him away playfully.

"And you have changed enough for both of us – when I left you were still a gangly child, constantly underfoot. Now I find you grown into a lovely young woman. Galerius must be pleased with you."

Julia's expression saddened. "I suppose you haven't heard. My father is not well, but I imagine he is proud of me. I don't always listen to him, but he is tolerant of my whims."

The whispers in the city had Galerius on his deathbed and Crispus changed his mind on feigning ignorance of the former emperor's fate. Julia deserved more than that from him. "How is your father? Indeed, I have heard that he is deathly ill but I didn't credit it. Can that be true?"

Julia was plainly shocked that he asked so personal question. A cool look returned to her face. "My father is not dying and I think it's inappropriate for you to ask such a question considering your own troubles. Have you forgotten where you are? This is his capital!" The words came out in a rush of anger.

"I am in my aunt's house and I'm not concerned about the judgments of others, especially men whose own histories are worse!" Crispus said, his anger rising to match hers. The conversation threatened to turn bitter, but Licinius arrived just then.

"Crispus, there are too many women here for just me! Come, let us –" Licinius abruptly stopped when he realized Julia was glowering as though she might kill one of them.

Crispus for one was happy for the interruption. "Where were you hiding? I have been searching for you." Crispus asked him. After the near debacle he had just made of his first encounter with Julia, he eagerly to move on.

"I've been chasing girls around this party, cousin. Where else would I be? There's too much beauty here to do otherwise, most of it untouched. But I see the most enticing is right before me. Julia! It has been too long. How are you, love?" He kissed her on each cheek and wrapped her in a quick embrace.

Julia squirmed away with a giggle. "Licinius, you're a menace. Ply your trade somewhere else. Your charms are lost on me!"

"Are they?" he quizzed with a raised brow.

Crispus watched the exchange between them. It reminded him of the easy friendship they shared as children. The passing years diminished none of it. As more guests flooded the vestibule and atrium, they shifted to an adjoining hallway where it was quieter.

"Absolutely – they're lost on me," Julia said in answer to Licinius' mocking question. "The other girls may flow like rivers to the lowest point, but I'm a bit more discriminating in my tastes." Nose held high, she sniffed in Licinius general direction.

"And I'm a croc, snapping them up whole." Licinius mocked without shame. He fairly gleamed with the prospect of the debauchery and secret delights that lay in store for him. "I just have to choose the right one. That's the trickiest part of the game because they usually warn each other about me."

"And well they should…" Crispus said, joining in the discussion. He stopped a passing serving girl to take a cup of mulsum for each of them.

"I pity these poor, love-starved creatures. I know most of them. Perhaps I should go warn them myself and save them the trouble!" Drink in hand, Julia started to do just that, before Crispus stopped her.

"You know Licinius, he's only talking. He's just trying to fluster you. And besides," he told her, "You can't escape me that easy – not without a kiss!" Laughing, he seized her and planted a kissed on her forehead. Julia poked him in the side and squirmed away.

"Save your kisses for your horse!" Julia called out over her shoulder. She went back to the party, shaking her head at the antics of her old friends. Crispus and Licinius watched as she flitted between groups of partygoers, including men. The men moved closer to her as she talked with them. Her casual flirtations did not bother Crispus in the least. He understood the fascination with her, he was a susceptible as the others.

Julia was beset on all sides by ambitious suitors. After careful thought, Crispus decided for some of them, intense interest in her sprang at least in part, from her proximity to her father's treasury. A sharp blade and skilled hands to wield it, suited Julia better than the womanly arts of poetry and seduction. Yet the men flocked about her. The small amount of restraint any of them showed was due to Crispus.

Most people there knew of his history with Julia and of his reputation in battle. No man wanted problems with him. And so her admirers were bold, but not too bold as to rile the guest of honor.

For now, he watched her, and he was not alone. The other unattached females were coiled little vipers, nested in small groups, surveilling Julia, and whispering mean-spirited little comments on her simple stola and her minimal styling. They noted everyone watching her, despite her appearance and scowled all the more.

Crispus was torn away from the game by a tap on his shoulder and Zenobia's handmaid Adelpha appeared at his side. "There is another visitor here; a woman who demands to see you. She was shouting curses at you from the streets, crowds were gathering. The doorkeeper let her in to keep her quiet. She's waiting in the vestibule." She lowered her voice and her eyes. "A peaceful removal without seeing her may not be possible, she's surrounded by bodyguards. The domina says if she is asking for you, then you should deal with her. And to do it quickly."

Crispus gaped at her. He felt his stomach drop as though a weight landed in the pit of it. *It's not possible.* How could she have found him here?

He said the name with dread. "Is her name Cassia?"

"Yes, I believe that is what she said. She demands to see you and says she will not leave until she does."

Adelpha pointed behind him, Crispus moved to a darkened corner of the room and spied on the vestibule from it. Through the circle of guards, a girl stood with her back to him, examining the wax effigies of his mother's ancestors. She was dressed in a gauzy red stola that clung in just the right places. Her hair sat atop her head in golden blonde loops which threatened to break free of the ruby combs that held them. The stola dipped low behind her, accentuating the arch of her back and the curve of her hips. He felt a familiar stirring within him, yet he approached her with caution. Once injured, a tigress can never be trusted again. As he came closer, he noticed a subtle shift in her and she straightened her shoulders. She sensed him but made no move to acknowledge him.

"Cassia." Just her name, she startled but did not turn. Evidently she recognized his voice and wanted to play her usual games. Her guards were in on her plans. They looked the other way and did not stop him from getting closer to her.

At this, Crispus placed his hand firmly at her waist, turning her to him. Her catlike eyes narrowed and her pouty little mouth formed the smirk he had come to know so well. *She's enjoying this*, he thought annoyed as he frequently was with her. *Everything is play with this woman!* Crispus steeled against an impulse to return her to the street himself. Cassia would like nothing better than another chance to embarrass him in front of his guests.

"Cassia, what a surprise, I was not expecting you," he said tightly. His hand clamped down on her shoulder hard even as his lips formed words of welcome he did not mean.

Cassia paid no heed. She smiled brightly at Crispus, as though they had parted the best of friends. "Well, if I lost have your interest, at least I have won your attention tonight. Don't be rude, Crispus. Greet me properly."

She removed his hand from her shoulder and held her own hand out to him. Crispus had no choice but to take it and kiss it, despite his deep reservations. When he dropped it, Cassia seized the opportunity to toss her arms about his neck. She crushed her mouth onto his, kissing him deeply in front of everyone, and leaving no doubt there was a relationship between them.

Crispus was dumbstruck. He allowed the kiss, even as the other guests gaped at the brazen act. Some older people looked away in abject embarrassment and shock. One person who did not look away was Julia. her body was rigid and trembling. She stopped listening to the nobleman whispering in her ear. Crispus and Cassia had her full attention.

At last Crispus found his wits. He pulled away from Cassia's embrace. Her laughter resounded in his ears as she spun away and headed into the atrium. Behind her, Crispus scanned the crowd, hoping Julia had not witnessed the encounter, but he knew otherwise the moment his found her face among the sea of guests.

To Crispus it was as though all the air had been sucked from the room. The revelers around him faded into the background. Anger and pain made Julia's eyes appear beady, they remained focused on him alone. Crispus felt hot, flushed with blood rushing to his head. Julia's expression told him she was as betrayed by the sight as she was by Cassia's outrageous kiss that caused it. He would have given all the gold in Saturn's treasury for Julia not to have witnessed Cassia's display. Yet, she had seen it, and he dreaded what the consequence would be.

In a blind rage, Crispus went after Cassia, determined to make her pay for her recklessness. He caught up to her in a hallway, near a spare cubicula[11] by chance left open. Before she could flee again, he snatched her by the arm, trundled her into the room and shut the door behind them. Cassia was mute, and all the while she kept up the satisfied smirk Crispus had come to know so well. It infuriated him; he abandoned all pretenses of nicety.

"You little wench!" He was seething, his body posed to threatened harm. "Whatever game you think you're playing here, it's not working. You just made a fool of us both! We are done. Why don't you just stop this?"

"So you say, but I think seeing me is not so terrible as you would like to pretend. There was no lie in your kiss, Crispus, or in mine. You still feel something for me. Don't deny it – even in the presence of your little girl out there. Don't think I didn't see her, watching us. She was the only one near tears at our embrace. Quite obvious, I must tell you. You should train her better." She glowered at him. "She's pretty, but she's not quite me – is she?"

"By you, I suppose you mean whorish and cunning? Because she surpasses you in both looks and spirit. Add to that she's Galerius' daughter, and I don't think you want to start this war, do you, Cassia? We had a little fun together, nothing more. Why can't you see that and stay in your place…where you should be?"

"Keep telling yourself that, Crispus, maybe

---

[11] Proper name for Roman bedrooms

you'll start to believe it." With that, she wrenched open the door. Leaving him there, she moved to the main triclinium where actors were performing Seneca's *Hercules Furens*. Within sight of Crispus, Cassia stopped near the actor portraying the vengeful Juno, hellbent on driving Hercules, the hero mad.

Crispus stood in blank wonderment. *That woman is a force of nature, nothing scares her,* he thought. In the recesses of his mind, where thought was beyond his control, there was a sliver of admiration. Cassia was brash, unapologetic and determined to have what she wanted regardless of consequence, qualities he shared with her. Nonetheless, he was no lovestruck Hercules, foolish enough to allow a female to drive him insane. He returned his thoughts to Julia, who disappeared while Cassia occupied his attention. Crispus knew just where to look for her.

As expected, he found her in the peristyle garden. Since childhood, Julia had a passion for plants and animals. When she was a girl coming to visit with Zenobia, she would beg his aunt to allow her to help her care for the gardens. They made quite the pair, two noble women in unadorned tunics, elbow deep in dirt and smelly growing treatments. It was a happy place for Julia; one she would surely run to for solace if she was upset.

Julia was resting on a stone bench, barefoot with her sandals tossed casually beside her. A heated wading pool lay before her, and she leaned over it, watching her reflection ripple as she teased the water with her feet.

Crispus approached tentatively, he sat beside her. "This was once your hiding place – do you remember? You thought the blooms and bushes would hide you from Licinius and me."

Julia shifted away from him. "I wish they could hide me from you right now. Can't you see I'd rather you weren't here? Go away."

Crispus tried again. "You blame me for things beyond my control. I couldn't stop Cassia, but she's nothing more than a bad memory come back to haunt me."

"Oh, is that the trollop's name? I wondered. With such a garish stola and overpainted face, I thought she was a streetwalker who followed a customer into the house. She should do well tonight in that case; I assume you're one of the better-paying deviants."

Crispus smiled in spite of himself. "That's not fair, to me at least. Truthfully, I've had occasion to suspect the same, but she's no common prostitute. In Ariminum, her family is held in high regard."

"We are far from Italy. Here she is just an upstart peasant with the moral fortitude of a bitch in heat." The venom she spewed contorted her mouth, marring Julia's otherwise delicate features. Crispus was at a loss for how to deal with her. When he left for war, she had been just a silly girl, but now she was a woman, full of the jealousy and means that came naturally to her sex. Crispus could not help his quiet amusement.

"So I'm a joke to you, even now," she said, but there was no anger in it. Instead, she sounded sad.

"No, Julia. Forgive me. The sight of you sitting here, with your feet dangling makes me recall the other times you sat on this bench because of some injustice on my part. It shamed me to see you so then, and it still does now. I need you to know that

I've come to Nicomedia for two purposes, and I stay…" He stopped short of telling her about the days and nights he spent thinking about ways to reconcile with her. He wanted to spill his heart out to her, but the words would not come. He forced himself to act. She had already rejected him, he told himself. The best time to risk it all is when there is nothing left to lose.

"Julia, I -"

She stopped him with a look. "You stay to torture me when decency; if you had any, would call you to leave me alone." Julia straightened her back. She focused all her attention on the statues around her, their curves, the way the vines crawled across them, anything to avoid his gaze.

Crispus waited, studying her in an intimate way. After a time, she turned to peek at him and found him still watching. Crispus moved closer to her but was silent. Julia lost her patience with him.

"Speak or go!" she whispered harshly to him. She tightened her grip on the bench, her knuckles turned white with the effort.

"You don't have to be this way with me. I mean you no harm. You are still my dearest friend," he said quietly.

"And nothing more – that much is clear to me now. Nor will I ever be. That is clear as well. I came here tonight because I fooled myself into believing that your invitation was an apology. I see now it was just a lure, to give you the chance to ridicule me as you once did. I don't believe you about that woman.

After your 'passionate' kiss, she turned to me, her damn smirking face told the whole tale. Goodnight Crispus. I'm going to find better company and don't try to follow me!" She grabbed up her sandals and made to leave the garden.

As she stepped onto the path, Crispus called after her, with as much nastiness as he could muster sitting in a beautiful garden arguing with an equally beautiful woman, "Other company? Licinius perhaps, as he was in the past? You'll find his company missing tonight, I'm afraid. He's otherwise occupied with fresh prospects."

Julia stopped in her tracks, shocked into stillness by the accusation he hurled at her. She turned back to face him.

She spoke low, in untapped fury. "You forget yourself. How dare you speak to me so? I tell you now as I told you then. Licinius is a brother to me. We would not betray that for anything or anyone, including you!" With that, she ran off down the path and disappeared into the shadows of the villa.

Crispus lingered on the bench, wishing he had kept his mouth shut about Licinius and Julia. He did nothing more than remind both of them of worse times. Licinius was a problem years ago and he was still a problem in the present.

And all of it a result of the portentous night, Julia professed her love to him. Crispus rejected her and Licinius consoled her as a brother, or that was the story they stood by about that night. Crispus had long wondered if there was more to it, but in the face of their denials and his pride, he had no choice but to leave it alone.

"I suppose I'll never know." Crispus sat in the empty peristyle nursing his troubled thoughts until the candles around the now gloomy peristyle sputtered low and extinguished. His mind was still reeling, but he returned to the remnants of the party. Julia was nowhere to be found by the time he reappeared, but Cassia lingered, engaged in deep conversation with his Aunt Zenobia.

Crispus overheard Cassia agreeing to Zenobia's offer to stay the night. He hoped she would find distraction with the house boys and leave him alone. After her antics earlier, he wanted to keep as far from her as possible. The idea came to him to unleash Licinius on her. He would be sure to give her what she wanted and more. Happy to have a solution to the Cassia problem, Crispus went to seek Licinius out but like Julia, he was missing from the party.

Chapter Eight

The Summons

The following morning, Crispus awoke with images of the night before playing through his mind. Dark, lustful visions he was ashamed to remember in the light of day. Beside him, the rounded indentation left by Cassia in his bed caught his attention. She had come to him, insatiable, just before dawn and later slipped out of his room with as much stealth as she entered it. His latest adventure with her began when she broke his sleep with her tongue flickering below his waist. In the early dawn hours, his defenses were low, his morale even lower and doing bad things with a bad woman was the most natural choice in the world.

He could not blame her for this one. It was his fault and he knew it well. The more he thought about what he had gone with her, the more shame he felt about it. Crispus pushed aside his blankets and headed straight to the baths, cursing himself for a fool the whole way there.

I should have thrown her out. It was a refrain that played in endless circles in his mind. He kicked the walls outside the bath, frightening the attendant and earning himself a sore foot in the process. When he emerged an hour later, he should have felt refreshed, but the stubborn layer of regret and guilt did not wash off so easily as the other traces of Cassia. He vowed again that he was done with her.

Whether from disgust or hunger, his belly gave an unpleasant lurch. He went to join the household for the morning meal. When he reached the triclinium, he found to his surprise that Julia was already there, sitting close beside Licinius with nary a hair's width between them. Licinius was the first to acknowledge him. He greeted Crispus with bleary eyes while Julia averted hers altogether, choosing instead to busy herself plucking figs from her fruit salad.

Crispus, now under the sway of his worse inclinations and emotions felt a stab of anger at the scene. He directed his irritation at Julia first. "I thought you left with your mother since there was only bad company here last night? I see you changed your mind."

The snippy way he said it made Julia freeze, her hand stuck in midair as she plucked a fig. She looked up then and matched his gaze with an icy one of her own. Her eyes fell to the bright red welt on the side of his neck; there was no question what it was and who gave it to him. "I did think to leave after that shabby display, but mother wanted me to stay, so I did." She turned away from him in disgust and went back to plucking figs.

"She was in the cellar. I found her among the amphorae, sobbing," Licinius said, wading into the fray unasked. For once Licinius was not the comic relief of a problem. He was uncomfortable and it showed. He shifted awkwardly and slid away from

Julia as though anticipating trouble.

Julia bristled, snapping at Crispus. "He did nothing but offer comfort." Licinius visibly relaxed when she did not offer details, instead she changed the subject. "–And, it was not the first time we have found ourselves in a cellar, if you remember. We talked all night and split an amphora of Sestian between us, although Licinius had the greater part of it judging by his bedraggled appearance this morning."

"You must speak more softly. My head is pounding hard enough to wake the dead," Licinius added, back to himself after his momentary awkwardness.

"So the two of you were up all night…talking?" Crispus asked with a note of sarcasm.

Julia was not bothered in the slightest by his tone. Instead, she matched it. "Of course. What else? A better question is what you were doing last night that earned you that mark on your neck? Did the bed ticks get to you or something worse?"

"My guess is something worse –" Licinius offered, rubbing his temples. "I'm just telling truths." He said in his own defense when his commentary was met with stony silence.

Before Crispus could give him the nasty response he deserved, a clerk appeared. "A visitor from the court in Mediolanum requests an audience sir," he said, addressing Crispus.

The news surprised each of them, but it was Licinius who broke the spell.

"Pick up your jaw from the floor, Crispus! Uncle Constantine finds your head too empty to call for it again."

Crispus was not amused. "Who asks for me?" he said to the clerk.

"He did not give his name. He only said that he must speak with you immediately concerning your grandmother."

Crispus could make no sense of it. "My grandmother? What fresh trouble is this? Bring him to me."

When the clerk returned escorting a familiar face, Crispus thought his eyes deceived him. His unexpected visitor was none other than Anthimus, Lactantius' trusted servant. Crispus had last seen him in Laus Pompeia, half a world away and a lifetime ago it seemed. Whatever he had to say would be substantial, of that Crispus had no doubt.

"Anthimus! What on earth are you doing here? Where is my grandmother? Is she safe?"

"She's still in Armenia. Her safety is why I'm here. She's no longer in Armenia as a guest of King Tiridates. He's keeping her as a hostage, at the bidding of Maximinus Daia no less. He's allied with Maxentius in Rome and Tiridates is hoping to curry favor with the Eastern rulers. Your grandmother is afraid of making the conflict worse if her captivity is revealed. Constantine would have to go to war with Daia, or risk the world knowing he couldn't protect his own mother. But that is not why she sent me to you. She would not have either you or your father put at risk for her."

Crispus dropped his head to his hands. "This must not be! What does he ask for her freedom?"

"Maximinus does not send terms of release to you. In fact, he does not know that I have spoken with her at all. I would never have been in Armenia except that Lactantius entrusted me to deliver vital information to her. When I reached her, I found her in bad circumstances of her own. She refused to talk about a release. She was more concerned about you and your father."

"She's unharmed then?" Crispus asked.

"Yes, she is quite well. She asks you to come to her, if you can. She has items of great importance that she must give to you herself."

"Of course. Thank you Anthimus, you're a true friend."

Julia shook her head. "Well, I'm not surprised. Helena has not changed at all. Forever concerned for others when her own head is far from safe." She clapped her hands together. "When do we leave?"

Crispus' answer was immediate and firm. "We," he emphasized, waving a hand around the table, "–Are not going anywhere. Licinius and I will leave for Armenia at first light, and you will go home, or stay here with Aunt Zenobia if you like."

Julia was having none of it. "You're a madman if you think I'll stay behind in Nicomedia! You need me, and so does Helena. I'm better with a blade and a better archer than most of the men in your army, which you don't have right now anyway."

"She has a point. She beat both of us more times than I can count when we were children," Licinius admitted.

"Licinius, do please be quiet! We are not children now. It's too dangerous for Julia, and you know it. And while the risk is acceptable to us, it is not for her. When…"

Licinius gestured at Julia and interrupted him,

"–Do you not see that you're fighting a losing battle, cousin? Look at her! She will have her way." Julia's face was set in hard determination. She was not a woman to be denied.

"I see her." Crispus muttered bitterly, resigning himself to a fight.

A silent match of wills ensued between them. Licinius went on despite their standoff. "I want to know why Daia is bothering to hold her in the first place? He must know Constantine will not yield but this insult is sure to bring a swift answer."

"Is her freedom not prize enough for him to take her and for us to free her?" Crispus argued bitterly. He turned his attention away from Julia and to his cousin.

"Slow down, Crispus. That's not what I meant. Of course we're going to free her – Helena is like a grandmother to me, but I wonder what else might be part of this, that's all." Licinius said quickly, putting up his hands to diffuse his angry cousin.

With a well-timed cough, Anthimus brought them back to his reason for being there. "Daia and Tiridates have her because they think she's holding something of great value, a relic of some sort. She denies it of course but he does not want to risk Constantine gaining an advantage. He's keeping Helena's capture a secret. If he can take you as well, so much the better. I was with Lady Helena under disguise for several days where they're holding her. I can draw a map for you but you'll need to tread carefully and keep your visit a secret from all. She's not in any immediate danger. Even Daia won't harm an old woman."

"What? And leave her there to rot? Surely not.

I'll take my chances. Daia will not dare strike at Licinius, me and hold my grandmother. He would have both our fathers descend on him with fire and slaughter."

And with that one remark, Crispus himself supplied the reason for Julia to join them. "And when you add the daughter of Galerius to the party, Daia would be a fool to try anything reckless. You need me. Just admit it."

Crispus still refused. "Your family won't allow it. We'll be hunted the moment we set foot on the road with you. Be reasonable, Julia! This is not a game. I told you, it's too dangerous. You cannot possibly go with us. Don't press the issue further."

"You don't remember me at all if you think you can dissuade me with a few words. I'm coming with you, and you should not press *me* further!" She stormed away, leaving the men to gape after her.

"Women!" Crispus muttered, reaching for her abandoned fruit salad. He was suddenly starving. "She doesn't know what she's asking." With that, he dismissed the notion of Julia and her stubborn ideas. He had other things to consider, whether or not Julia had lost her mind was not one of them.

"Take some food and drink, Anthimus. Tell us how you came to be in Armenia. When last we saw you, you were in Laus Pompeia with Lactantius. I want to know everything. Please!"

"It's an interesting tale and an adventure I must share…" Anthimus laughed and made himself comfortable with his old friends now that his mission was complete. Few things are as satisfying as a job well done, good food and even better friends to share it with him.

"Too dangerous, humph! He has nerve lecturing me about danger when he's been running for his life for months!" Julia went home in a blind rage, muttering curses the entire litter ride home. That Crispus would discount her that way was unfair and insulting. Her sex had never mattered to her. She never asked quarter from any man, nor did she expect it.

She doubted worry over her was the real reason for his refusal. His behavior of the past night came back to her in a rush. Women were handy enough for some things apparently, judging by the mark on his neck. She thought of the kiss she watched him share with Cassia, and his pretending he did not enjoy her. There was something in the way his arms had come around her before he snatched away that betrayed the truth. Crispus was just ashamed to be around her now that she knew about Cassia.

But none of that mattered. She was going, and that was the end of it. Back at the imperial palace, she raced about her room, throwing things all around, she gathered the few things she would take on the journey. She packed a cloth travel bag lightly, Crispus would be looking for any excuse to stop her and too many traveling clothes would do nothing except weaken her already tenuous relationship with him.

Julia felt a pang of guilt when she thought of her father. Galerius was failing more each day, and she did not expect he would be among the living much longer. Julia could only imagine how he would react when he learned she had run away with men from the house of Constantius Chlorus. Although their houses were politically connected, Galerius had abhorred the man. Julia did not think he would die at the news, or she would not go, but just the same, he was not likely to ignore her rebellious act. He was likely to send men to drag her back home. Julia's only hope was to get far enough away from Nicomedia that chasing her down would be a daunting task.

"You returned much later from Zenobia's house than expected Julia. Explain yourself. I told you come home at first light." Julia turned to see her mother standing in the doorway of her chamber, still clad in her morning robes with her arms folded across her chest, an unhappy scowl on her face.

"Oh mother, do stop it! I'm sure you've already heard from your spies about what happened last night…or what did not. I'm home and everything is fine." Julia said forcefully, hoping to avoid an argument with her mother if she could.

There was no such luck for her this morning, Galeria confronted her just the same. "That's not all I hear – did you think you could keep it a secret from me? Or that I will permit you to scandalize our name while your father lies dying?"

Anger rose in Julia's voice as well. "I scandalize nothing! I don't know what you're going on about mother, but I have done nothing wrong. I simply lingered in the house of old friends, old friends you insisted I see! You're overreacting…as usual."

"Lies. I know you spent the night in a cellar with Emperor Licinius' son alone, like a common strumpet. What were you thinking? Our good name means nothing to you. Do you deny it?"

"I do. Now leave me alone, please."

"And I suppose you also deny you're trying to leave our home, abandon all you know and love to play the consort? Did you really think your little audience with that visiting slave had gone unnoticed? My eyes follow you everywhere."

"Not everywhere. Your sources are well placed but ill-informed. It shames me for you to be so foolish!" Julia turned her back on her mother.

Galeria's reaction to Julia's disrespect was swift. She seized Julia by the shoulders, spinning her around. Her stinging slap caught Julia by surprise. She recoiled from her mother. Galeria's unusual behavior unsettled the girl. A sliver of fear broke through Julia's façade of ambivalent detachment. She dropped her shoulders. "Mother, please just trust my judgment. I've done nothing to disgrace myself or you."

Galeria relented. "Some bits could be fabrications; I'll give you that. You're planning something. Just look at all this chaos!" She gestured around her. "–And the way you've spoken to me, your mother is completely unacceptable. You're not yourself and I would know the reason. Tell me what you're doing. We must rely on each other, who else do we have?"

"You're afraid of being alone. You miss Father as he once was and Valeria too. Now you think I'm leaving you too. But that's not what I'm doing."

"Child, will you continue to lie to my face?" Julia's denials were wearing on her mother and yet Julia could only stay with her story. "Enough. Valeria is a married woman with her own household and it is not your father I'm concerned about now, it's you.

Tell me the truth! You will never succeed without my help, and you know it. Continue to upset me with these lies, and see your chances wither, whatever this is, will fail."

Her mother was right, of course. Julia's ridged stance melted away. She moved away from her mother to sit on her open windowsill overlooking the rolling grounds of the palace complex. Julia sighed heavily and stretched out her legs catlike on the richly colored cushions. She was the image of confused innocence itself and the vision of her broke Galeria's resolve as well. She came to stand behind Julia and stroked her hair.

"My poor lamb. The burden is too heavy for your shoulders to carry alone. Let me be your mother, tell me what's going on with you, please."

"If I tell you, you will help me truly?" Julia asked in a small voice.

"I will do everything within my power," Galeria assured her. She could see Julia was still not entirely convinced. "Who can you trust in this world if me?"

At last, Julia told her the truth. "Helena Augustus is trapped in Armenia as a hostage. She's asked Crispus to come to her and he and Licinius leaving at first light. I'm going with them. Crispus tried to talk me out of it. He says it is too dangerous for me, but my mind is made up. I'm going."

Galeria was confused. She tried to reason with Julia. "But why should you take up his cause? I know you care about Helena, but what possible use can you be in this? Let Helena's family resolve the matter. Why not stay here at your father's…and my side."

Julia exclaimed, "I knew you wouldn't

understand! It is not too dangerous! I am as capable with a bow as any man, better than some. Besides, Valeria did not stay at Father's side. You and he sold her to Maxentius when you knew she hated him. Should I stay here to suffer a similar fate? My destiny is outside Nicomedia. I think I have always known that. Now when opportunity presents itself, you cannot expect me to turn away from it. Never! I'm leaving with Crispus and Licinius, and I don't give two figs about what anyone thinks about it. Help me if you wish mother, but don't try to stand in my way."

Galeria was flabbergasted. "What are you talking about, child? If Crispus and his cousin don't want your help, what more is there to say? You would defy everyone who loves you simply to have your way? Crispus will just leave without you and not waste precious time arguing the point."

"No, he won't. He remembers how stubborn I can be when I latch onto an idea. My only concern is Father, and you, if you insist on making a fuss. I don't want to spend my life tending to the hearth and home. I want to do something more with the time I have than wish for better days."

Something in Julia's tone struck Galeria. She grew reflective. "You know, when I was your age, I wanted to be an actor and travel the world entertaining people. It was impossible outcome of course, but what has always bothered me is I never thought enough of my dreams to ask the question."

She went on. "My father placed the same constraints on me you that are strangling you. Worse maybe, Diocletian was the originator of the tetrarchy. I had absolutely no say in who I would marry or where I would live. I agreed because it didn't occur to me to refuse. Purely by accident, I've reared a girl who knows she can say no. Believe it or not, that's something that makes me proud. You think I pay no attention to your feelings, to the things you're going through as a young woman forced into someone else's expectation for your life.

But, my dear heart...I see you. I breathe the same suffocating air that you breathe, I know the drive in your spirit that wants more than the world says you can have. I know you're restless and unhappy. And if you are so sure your future lies beyond Nicomedia–" She paused for a just a moment. "–Well then, you shall have your pleasure."

Julia blinked at her mother in bewilderment, she was dumbstruck. Never did she imagine her mother would agree to let her leave with her friends. She struggled to understand. "I'm grateful, so very grateful, but why the change of heart, mother?"

"Because you're right. You deserve your chance at the life you want. If it is to be outside Nicomedia, so be it. The fates are crueler to women than men. Married off to who knows who, like cattle to the highest bidder. I could not save myself or your sister, but perhaps there is a chance for you."

"I thought it was impossible for anyone else to know how I have felt, crawling through this life waiting to die, when all I want to do is feel alive! Thank you! Thank you! I won't betray the trust you have placed in me."

"And I hold you to that promise and one other – that you return to me."

"I will. Nothing but death will ever keep me from you!"

Galeria laughed bitterly. "That's what I'm

afraid of my dear love. Return to me as you leave me, in one piece and with your virtue intact. Can you promise that much?"

"Why do you ask that? I am leaving with my closest friends in the world. They would never let any harm come to me or force me to do anything I didn't want to do."

"No, the concern isn't them. It's you and your tendency to allow emotion to sweep you off to places you shouldn't go. Your father will be livid when he learns of this, but I will do this for you on one condition. I want to be able to tell him that you will return the better for it and without dishonor."

"I promise." Even as she vowed, Julia wondered if she could really keep it and if she even wanted to – this was her adventure and her time to grow beyond being just the emperor's wayward daughter. Her mother was missing some details about her and that was good.

Galeria stood, pulling Julia to her feet along with her. "Come," she said. "I have something for you."

Galeria took Julia to her private quarters, a lavish affair of exotic colors and textures. Wall hangings from Egypt, lion and zebra skin rugs, heavy tables and couches of precious cedar and ivory, and yards of intertwining silk and linen drapes that edged the tall, sunlit windows. At a nod from Galeria, the servant girls milling about the room, straightening Galeria's oversized bed and dusting the ornaments, left en masse.

In an inconspicuous corner in the back of the room sat a chest with open double doors and several rows of drawers. Galeria dug through gold jewelry and ornamental trinkets while Julia waited on the bed in rising curiosity. Galeria searched until she reached the lowest drawer and withdrew a small bundle which she unwrapped to reveal a beautiful fibula. It was unlike any Julia had seen before. The ornament was exceedingly old, made from wrought gold and so jewel encrusted that it gleamed like fresh ice in winter. The gold clasp was shaped into a delicate semicircle intricately etched in lines and whirls. Galeria handled it with extreme care, laying it in Julia's palm then closing her own over it.

"This was my grandmother's fibula that she received from her mother and her grandmother before her and on back for 300 years. The story is that it saved your great-grandmother Prisca's life once. I don't know if that is true. My mother loved stories, but she called it blessed. It has been passed on to only the worthiest females in the family. Your sister believes she will have this and the stipend that comes with it, but I give it to you and take from you a promise – that you will earn it."

With a great deal of humility, Julia accepted the fibula and the responsibility that came with it. "But why give this to me now?"

"Because the women in this family live in gilded cages, and you have the will to break free of yours. My grandmother would be proud. I know that. And wherever your path takes you, know that your family goes with you. Return to me with no regrets."

Galeria wrapped Julia in a loving embrace, stroking her hair as she had when Julia was a small girl. They stood that way with Julia locked within her mother's arms, relishing the feel of her love enveloping her. She had not felt this close to her in many years. Suddenly a thought occurred to her.

"Mother, how do you come to have the fibula? I mean no offense, I'm just curious."

Galeria's chuckle lightened the mood. "Well, if you must know, marrying your father was considered duty enough!"

As promised, the following dawn found Crispus, Licinius and Donatus in the stables readying their horses for their journey. Anthimus came down with them. He was leaving for Mediolanum and would share the road with them from the city. As promised, he gave Crispus a map leading him to his grandmother's location in Armenia.

Donatus had made fast friends with Licinius' man Quintus, a hearty sort of fellow recruited from the ranks of the unemployed veterans in Nicomedia. Having him along would be wise, Crispus thought. The further east they ventured, the more dangerous it would be for them.

For all his worry about Julia, Crispus knew he had Viatoro to consider as well. The stallion had arrived in Nicomedia as tired and ragged as his master. Crispus could not help feeling guilty for all Viatoro had endured over the past few months because of him. When he reached Viatoro's stall, he gave him a close once-over. The stallion was thinner to be sure, but had lost none of his vitality and his fighting spirit was intact. He stamped about in his stall, restless and impatient to be outside.

Crispus grabbed a nearby brush. He rubbed it across the golden brown silk of Viatoro's mane. "Easy old friend, you'll be running in the open air soon enough."

Licinius had been busy selecting from the available mounts in the stable, but now he came over to stroke Viatoro beside Crispus. "You're not alone in that, Viatoro. A few weeks of loafing around here are enough to make any creature long for an open road and wind at his back."

Crispus laughed. "So now you have something in common with my horse. More likely, his rear end – I heard a few girls call you a horse's ass after the party."

Licinius pretended shock. "You're one to talk, Crispus. That was Cassia I saw tip-toeing out of your rooms the next morning, was it not? I hope you bedded her well. I wish I'd gotten to her first!"

Crispus blushed deeply. "Fine, I won't deny it. She caught me at a weak moment. I will say this for her, she plays her game better than most. I did not even have to throw hints at her to make her leave. I couldn't imagine any other girl doing that. Thank how Julia would have reacted if I asked her to leave right after bedding her? I would still be removing her claws from my face!"

"You wouldn't have treated Julia that way, nor would she have allowed it. You can lie to yourself but not me. You would have welcomed her with open arms into your bed, and you know it."

Crispus could only smile. "Maybe."

As if summoned by their words, Julia appeared in the stable doorway. "I thought I would find you two here. Is everything in order then?"

Had it not been for her voice and her smile they would not have known her. Julia had transformed herself into a scruffy traveler with cropped hair, an oversized tunic and leather breeches fit for a hunter. There was a layer of grime on her face and her nails were cut short.

Crispus marveled at her. "You surprise me! How did you manage this? No one will suspect an emperor's daughter lurks beneath those rags!"

Julia gave him a knowing look. "I told you I could do it – now do you believe I can take care of myself?"

Licinius answered for him. "You look the part at least; we have to wait to see if you can play it too!"

Eager to change the subject, Crispus interjected. "I cannot fathom why your father and mother are allowing you to go with us. How you managed that is a bigger feat than this costume."

"It was Mother," Julia said. "I would not have thought it possible either, but she's proud of me. I'm going with her blessing, and she promises to tell father I'm visiting her cousin in Rome. He won't expect me back for months."

Crispus relented with a shake of his head at his defeat. "Fine, Julia. You win, as usual. I make no promises. We will send you home if you prove a burden instead of a blessing. Understood?"

Julia wrinkled her nose at his choice of words to describe her but she agreed. Crispus pulled a worn map from his bag. He spread it out on the floor of the stable. "Tell me what you think of this. I've plotted our route. Assuming the weather holds out, we should be in Armenia by mid-October."

Julia knelt in the dirt and muck of the stable

alongside the men. She examined the route, tracing it with her finger and repeating the cities and various mansios[12] Crispus had chosen along the way as resting places. "So we make for Yerevan, stopping along the way in – your handwriting is still terrible by the way – Caesarea Mazaca and Karin." Her finger stopped in its path; she nodded in approval. "I have traveled this route before with my family. It will take many days, but I think it's the best way given the circumstances. These roads you chose are trade routes, so they will be heavily populated. That will be helpful, and we avoid the mountains."

He grinned at her. "I'm glad you approve, then. Let us be off then, Grandmother is waiting for us."

Julia echoed him. "To Helena."

Licinius grabbed both of them in an embrace. "To Helena! Just as when we were children. She summons; we answer. Another adventure for the *terribilis tria*!"

"The terrible three," Julia said after him. "She called us that, didn't she? We'll soon see if she was right."

After the traveling party gathered their horses, and headed out of the city, there was someone left behind in the stable. Boteiras' body slave stepped delicately from behind the stable boy's quarters and raced off to report to his dominus. In his hand was a hastily scrawled list of the cities where Crispus and his friends would take refuge along the way to Armenia.

---

[12] An stopping place on a Roman road, an inn where travelers can rest and get fresh supplies

Chapter Nine

SPQR
(The Senate and People of Rome)

Rome – Senate House

Gaius Caeionius Volusianus pushed through the heavy bronze doors on the front of the Curia Julia[13] as though he owned the place, and in a way, he did. He was the Consul as well as acting Urban Prefect[14] or inside that building, God-on-High. Although Volusianus, a Christian, officially feigned humility at his position, in truth he relished his power. Every head turned in unison upon his arrival; attendants and sycophants rushed to greet him. He waved them away with a self-important flutter of his hand.

This morning Volusianus held his head a little higher than usual, walked with a longer stride. He was a man who held the emperor's ear, whose word set law, and the Senate would hear him today. He came from a long line of such men, and was a leader for other likeminded senators. Most were Christian leaning or flat out devotees with political agendas.

---

[13] The Senate house located in the Roman Forum, rebuilt after destruction by Julius Caesar and named after his family

[14] Magistrate charged with keeping the peace within the city

Confidence and an easy form of power radiated from him, palpable as smoldering flame, complimenting his handsome features, set hard with wide-apart, brown eyes and a square jaw underneath a well-maintained coif the color of charred wood.

His extravagant entrance into the chamber achieved its desired effect. The amassed Senate was duly intimidated, particularly his enemies, several of them portrayed a mask of such deliberate blankness, their envy was plainer than the dismissal and utter contempt they hoped to convey. Volusianus paid them little notice, his purpose for this session of the Senate was of too important to bother with small men and matters. At question was a proclamation to raise a levy for at least five new legions to aid Maxentius in his dispute against the usurper Lucius Domitius Alexander.

It was a tough sell. The Senate was bitterly divided right down the middle on the issue. There was little common ground. Hateful words had gone back and forth, and more than once – fisticuffs. The Christians Populares[15] in the Senate formed an effective voting bloc against Maxentius, a traditionalist or Optimate,[16] whose views of Roman dominance and duty to the pantheon of gods formed another bloc and those at the center, comprised of moderates of both faiths, kept balance between them. It was a curious beast they formed, one which the current turmoil threatened to kill in a self-

---

[15] Political party favoring the common people, and devoted to issues important to the urban poor and middle plebian class
[16] The old guard; the conservative, traditional party, a remainder from the Republican days of the senate.

administered avalanche of infighting and backbiting.

Domitius had been a loyal ally of Maxentius and his family for years, securing from them, the Praetorian Prefecture[17] in Africa, but seeing Maxentius take Rome had given him aspirations as it often does with men who know just enough to be dangerous. He rose up against Maxentius and seized control of the province. With control of North Africa, Domitius shut off the grain supply as suddenly as a tap, leaving Maxentius in a tough spot.

African grain was the only thing standing between Rome and starvation, and so Domitius' action in disrupting the supply had real consequences for Maxentius' leadership. The Christians pounced, decrying the cruelty but splitting on solutions while the Optimates railed against the costs. Unrest and protests grew as the people watched the grain supplies dwindle and the old and sick started dying. Unless Domitius was forced to release his hold over the grain supply, the city would descend into chaos.

It was no more than what Domitius hoped would happen. Control of Rome was his target. He turned away all of the emissaries Maxentius sent to negotiate with him and threatened to take their ears and geld from the next senator sent to beg for Maxentius. As Roman men were rather vain creatures, partial to their hearing and their manhood, this was naturally a serious hindrance to more volunteers.

An open fight was the only answer left, yet the overtaxed Optimates who wanted to see Maxentius fail would likely defeat the motion. His

---

[17] Head of the army in Africa and thus its ruler

only hope was to scrape together enough centralist senators and a few prominent Christians, Volusianus among them, to help him push the levy through the Senate.

And so Maxentius sent Ruricius and a clutch of well-armed tributes to lean on the noble man until he fell in line. With Rome and his own house on its knees, honor and duty demanded Volusianus align himself with Maxentius to break Domitius hold on the city. Domitius would not see reason, and Volusianus could see no alternative.

"Ahh, these are times that try the hearts of men," he sighed as he settled into the consul's chair, a seat his father had occupied many years prior. Across from him, the famed Altar of Victory[18] stood in stern-faced witness to the nefarious deeds that take place in the Curia. A symbol of Rome for over 500 years, the Altar had been in a place of honor during contentious, angry battles in the Senate before now.

Across from the Altar, the chair next to Volusianus sat empty. His fellow consul and occasional friend, Marcus Aradius Rufinus had not yet arrived. It was just as well; of late they had been at odds with each other. Volusianus could not allow the distraction today, his problems with Rufinus were small in comparison to the fate of Rome. His focus at the moment was on the largest obstacle to the plan, Senator Valerius Maximus Basilius. He was a charismatic, success-driven, fellow Christian with his own large following. Volusianus disliked him on sight. He had no doubt the feeling was mutual.

---

[18] Altar holding a golden statue of the goddess Victory that stood honored in the senate off and on from 29BC until 394

"Ah, there's the rascal now," he muttered to himself, rising from his seat. From the Consul's platform, he could see down the length of the chamber, pass the granite columns and white steps leading up the wide double doors at the front. He watched while Valerius Maximus Basilius swept into the chamber surrounded by his usual entourage of sycophants and pretty attendants. More heads turned towards him than Volusianus; not even an appearnace by Maxentius commanded so much attention.

Basilius was a man on the rise, buoyed by his own cunning and the ancient name he carried. The respect he received was given freely and not demanded at the end of a sword as so many around him. Volusianus could not help but wonder why Ruricius had not paid him the same visit, wondered why he as being made to grovel to Basilius instead.

Volusianus tried in vain to quell the rising tide of bitterness that formed in his throat at the sight of his rival. It was impossible to ignore the subtle change in the conversations around him, the boisterous glee he heard in the other men, just a little louder than it had been for him. "And they call themselves Senators of Rome, clucking about the man's skirts like newborn chicks," Volusianus mumbled, forgetting his own penchant for theatrics.

Without warning, a withered hand, falling on his shoulder interrupted his thoughts. "Do you know the plebs and some equestrians too, actually cry when he walks through the streets? They swoon as though he were Octavian Augustus or even Caesar himself, reborn. But just as Caesar, he is not to be trusted. Fortune favors us that he has no army behind him...yet." Old joints creaked aloud as the arm pulled away from his shoulder and the man rested it inside the folds of his toga.

Volusianus had not realized there was anyone close enough to hear him, but the bitterness in the voice matched his own. Volusianus did not need to turn around to know who touched him. None but Titus Postumius Titianus would speak to him so or do so while squeaking like an old door.

Titianus' advanced years and his shared status as former Consul and Urban Prefect permitted him liberties denied to less esteemed members of the Senate. What's more, Titianus was a true son of Rome. His family had been renowned since the great days of the Republic, and he expected the courtesy and respect his ancestry demanded. And like any old man he has been doing just as he liked for too long for anyone to bother him about it. He settled into Rufinus' seat as though it was his own.

Volusianus smirked at him in unsurprised wonder. "No army yet, but mark me the day is not long in coming. And when it does I fear he will become a true menace." Volusianus said with resignation and a heavy-shouldered sigh. He stood to embrace Titianus. "You received my message then. How are you, my friend? I thought you ill; you have not been in session for many months now."

"Yes, I have been sick, not in body as you might think but in spirit. I cannot bear to watch this sacred assembly my family has served for many generations descend into the muck. If not for this vote today, I would still be within the walls of my villa comfortable and safe in my ignorance. For once I agree with you Christians. The levy must pass!" A brief coughing fit took him just then. Volusianus waited polite and quiet for the elderly statesman to recover.

When he could breathe again, Titianus went on. "I have little regard for you Christians with your bleeding hearts for the people, but in this no decent man would sit idle. Without this levy, they will all starve. Our grain supplies are being depleted at an alarming rate, and when the city goes hungry; no one, rich or poor is safe in their home. We must open the treasury so that Maxentius can raise an army to put down this renegade in Africa and retake the province. You are in agreement with me?" It was supposed to be a question but it sounded more like a fervent statement of faith. His eyes lit fire-bright when he said it.

Volusianus answered with a passion that matched him. "We understand each other, though mine is under duress." Titianus raised a brow at this but Volusianus shook his head and refused to answer the unspoken inquiry; he went on.

"Many of my friends here are with me, would go to war, however reluctantly. But just as many want to see Maxentius fail, and to keep some peace before the storm, regardless of the cost to Rome. I told him he had to bring other moderate Christians to his side, but trying to sway them with Eusebuis' election as bishop was madness! Does he use his head at all? Everybody knows Eusebuis is Constantine's man. It makes him look weak and quick to grovel for the houses still tied to the Constantii rather than shrewd, as he might think it does."

He tutted in frustration the way a harried woman might about a wayward child. "Maxentius makes unwise decisions at every turn. Frankly, it's tedious trying to support him."

Titianus agreed but could only say "Be that as it may, we must do what we can."

"Well, we must have the support of Basilius if we are to have any chance of success. With both his family and the Septimii behind us, victory would be assured," Titianus said. He looked around at the milling senators. "Come, let us retire to another room where we can speak without appearing to conspire. We'll rejoin our colleagues once your friend Rufinus decides to make an appearance."

Volusianus looked again at Basilius with a petulant frown. "Anywhere, as long as that little peacock is out of my sight, for now."

The Curia Julia played host to more than just a meeting of the Senate. In another part of it, Maxentius worked toward the same goal as Volusianus though his methods were not as precise. Despite the importance of the day's vote, and the dire circumstances of the people, he had indulged in his usual debaucheries until late into the previous night. As was his practice since becoming emperor, he left the formation of a practical strategy to his generals, intervening only to settle the occasional squabble. Today he did it while nursed a raging headache, and instead of his imperial regalia, was clad in what could only be called a housecoat; it was completely inappropriate for a meeting of the Senate and Maxentius did not care one whit.

While Volusianus and Titianus petitioned on

Maxentius' behalf in the adjacent hall, General Ruricius did his best to ignore the emperor's disheveled appearance and keep to the business at hand. Maxentius rested his hand on his head, his fingers rubbing the beginnings of gray hair at his temple. He sat with his eyes closed. He opened them only to complain or reject an idea his men presented to him. The gathered senators and other allies grew frustrated, began to bicker with each other until Ruricius silenced all of them with a wave. He laid his hand on his emperor's shoulder. Maxentius barely registered the touch. Ruricius had to tap his shoulder a few times to get him to open his bleary eyes.

"Dominus…Sire! Listen to me. With or without the Senate behind you, we must raise more legions to stand against Domitius, even if we have to break into the treasury and take the gold ourselves. If we do not mount an offensive now with whatever forces we can muster, we may as well hand Rome over now and save ourselves the trouble of a fuss later. If this vote should go against you – seize the treasury by force."

"You advise our emperor to thieve the public resources? Before the eyes of the gods and the city? Blasphemy! The gods will turn from us, and if the people condemn his greed as well, they may open the gates to Constantine just to spite us," this from Felix, a respected strategist and Legate in Legio IV; he was a favorite of Maxentius. He was not usually permitted in such high meetings but given the dire situation Maxentius wanted anyone with a mind for war around him.

Ruricius scoffed. He dismissed Felix as he would a buffoon juggling apples, snapping at him,

"We can't trifle with imaginary concerns while our enemies gather around us!"

He turned to Maxentius, "Send an army to deal with Domitius by any means at your disposal and to hell with this childish banter!" He smashed his hand down on the arm of his chair with a loud clap.

Ruricius took a deep breath to calm himself. "This is the only rational thing to do. I'll head north to Verona to fortify the border against an invasion. With Constantine forced to concentrate on us, he can't come to Domitius' aid. We can divide their forces. You father's veterans are loyal to you. Make them all Evocati[19] and they will replenish the ranks I take with me to the North. Send our remaining forces to deal with Domitius. This are our best option, I daresay it's the only one with a route to victory."

Maxentius straightened in his chair and pulled his robe closer around him as though he were cold. "It's a feasible strategy, but what of the city? With my armies in the field, the city will not have adequate defenses, and the dangers from within are just as deadly as those from the outside. The damn Christians are stirring up trouble again. They will not be satisfied until there are riots in the streets! It's all too tiring to consider," Maxentius grumbled, earning him a flash of weary disgust from Ruricius that he missed but was seen by all the rest.

"Keep two of the most loyal legions here. That should be enough to guard the city," offered a junior officer.

Senator Titianus' son Primus spoke next.

---

[19] Retired soldiers who return to active duty at the special request of the emperor. Considered a high honor for a soldier

"What if Constantine lays siege? There is not enough food in the city, nor are two legions enough to defend it during a long engagement. My father knows how low the grain stores are already. He's on the floor arguing this very point. The situation is more dire than anyone can imagine."

"All the more reason to seize the treasury now. The sacrilege is not in raiding Saturn's treasury, it's in not doing everything possible to prevent our own demise. We need the grain ships moving again, and soon. " Ruricius added.

The group was unexpectedly interrupted when a young Senate aid rushed into the room, out of breath from his sprint. He stood at attention before Maxentius.

"Sire, the vote has been taken. The proposed legislation has been defeated. The Senate will not authorize a new levy."

Maxentius' drink-reddened face turned an even deeper hue at the news. He jumped to his feet. "What are you saying? They defy me while I stand in this Curia, a breath away?" He turned to Ruricius in anger. "You said the necessary votes had been secured, yet I find myself in this embarrassing defeat! How did you let this happen?" He shouted into Ruricius' face; spittle flying in all directions.

To his credit, Ruricius stood his ground. He waited calmly until the tirade was over with all the patience of a parent waiting out a child's tantrum. Then he spoke to his commander. "It had to be Basilius. He managed to secure votes we thought were safe. There was nothing more I could have done but we must move forward and not dwell on this defeat."

Maxentius refused to be pacified. He sputtered, "Not dwell on it? You lost the vote and my dignity with it! How will you return them to me, with empty words and promises? Tell me what you think you can do to turn back time in a room full of fools who take me for one if they believe I will spill no blood at this insult! Send someone to cut Basilius' throat for me!" Maxentius paced the room, enraged and without recourse, it streamed from him in near palpable waves.

Ruricius raised a hand to delay a courier from racing off with the intemperate order, "You cannot kill Basilius. He's too popular. Our allies in the Senate would run for cover screaming tyranny. If an untouchable man like Basilius can be killed, none of them are safe. They won't have it. It would not be the first time senators have risen up against their leader. No, until we are at full strength, we cannot touch him."

"Then what is to be done?" Primus Titianus asked in a tiny voice that would have shamed his proud father to hear.

Ruricius turned to him, his patience running out. "You speak like a frightened child! Are you a Roman or not? Basilius must be turned to our cause, and the vote revisited. Even the dullest of minds can see that."

Primus bristled at the insult, but a snap of Maxentius' fingers settled him down. Satisfied, Ruricius went on. "Basilius will soon see resisting you only makes problems for him. Trust me, Sire. Have I ever failed you before?"

"You haven't," Maxentius admitted.

"Know that I will not start now when the

need is most dire. We will have the gold for your campaigns and reclaim the lands the coward Domitius stole from you."

Maxentius held up a hand to stop him. His imperial signet ring squeezed his plump middle finger, grown swollen in his excesses, along with the rest of him. "Well and good...all that is well and good. But what of today? What will you do to address this humiliation, this open rebuke at the hands of a traitorous few?"

It was Felix who explained the situation best. "For the moment, Sire there is nothing you can do. The session has adjourned but you may call a new one in a few days. In the meantime, the point of a sword may persuade where words failed. Perhaps a nighttime visit to some of the opposition's homes?"

Maxentius nodded. "Do it – but be careful. These are Senators of Rome, any whisper they were harmed and the people will blame me. I have enemies enough, I need no new ones among the citizenry because I was caught murdering their beloved leaders."

A new thought occurred to Maxentius just then as they talked about his enemies. "About Charietto – Has there been any word on Constantine's son? I had hoped to have him in my hands by now. Or have you failed there as well." The jab was as unnecessary as it was sharp. Ruricius as usual ignored it.

"I had a report just this morning that Charietto has closed in on him. He's outside of Cappadocia, and he expects to take him soon, barring incident."

"See that he does – having Constantine's heir

in our hands improves our chances for victory.

Ruricius agreed. "My thoughts exactly," he said as he left to find Basilius.

Later that night, Maxentius appeared in his wife's rooms as Valeria prepared for bed. He had not spoken to her since leaving that morning, but there was no doubt she was aware of the outcome of the vote. She made her feelings clear right from the start by not acknowledge his presence at all, until Maxentius grew impatient with the theatrics.

"I do not care how upset you are, Valeria. I am still your emperor and your husband and will not tolerate this kind of insolence, even from you. If you have thoughts about what happened at the Curia today, then spill them and be done with it!"

Valeria whirled at her dressing table to face him. She had been having her hair brushed out but now she sent the girl away. Turned toward him, her dark beauty and exotic features were made more so by her anger. She threw him into confusion with the strenght of it. Her eyes were the stormy blue of an overcast day, they twinkled in a bewitching fashion, and her olive-toned cheeks flushed a deeper red than even the berries staining them could produce. Her raven hair rained in a black flood, straight and loose down her back.

It was only her words that were ugly. "You fancy yourself an emperor, do you? You shame the title! How can I hold my head above others as your empress when you bow and scrape so low? The

Senate defies you at every turn, mocking you. And how do you answer the insult? You take your defeat and slink away home, a cur dog with your tail safely tucked!"

Valeria strode over to him, she placed her face inches from his. "Tell me Maxentius, are these rebels in the Tullianum, awaiting the executioner? Are they being driven from the city like the criminals they are? No, they sit smug and warm in their homes with no fear of you. You are not an emperor or even a man anyone can respect!"

Maxentius looked past her to the slaves who prepared her chamber. "Leave us!" he ordered them. They dropped their work like surprised mice and scurried away leaving them alone together. Valeria was spoiling for the fight. She stood with her fist clinched at her sides, bold in her outrage and ready to do battle but still so beautiful she could stop his heart with a glance. It was impossible for him to remain angry with her.

Maxentius began in an attempt to pacify her, "Valeria, please…I have done what I could." He held his hands out to her, a penitent begging a merciful audience. It was a display sure to melt any heart except a wife who feels her husband is a fool. Maxentius tried nonetheless.

"Ruricius and I have crafted a plan. We intend to see both the treasury and the Senate into our hands and this city at your feet. You must be patient and trust me. I know what I am doing. I will not fail you. I promise."

"Do you truly believe that? Because I don't find your plans so convincing."

Maxentius grabbed his wife, he held her tight

within his arms. "If I did not love you so much, I would feed those words to you at the end of my sword…or something else." he growled. His lips traced along the curve of her jaw. He bit at her earlobe as lust stirred within him.

Still angry, Valeria would have none of it. She wriggled away from him. "Stop it! I'm speaking to you! You hold both our lives in your hands." She could not have been more insistent or more adorable had she stamped her little feet. Such was not her intent, but reality betrayed her. She was a beautiful woman with a grievance. It was hard to be taken seriously by a man who loved her without really knowing her.

Maxentius was accustomed to Valeria's fits of temper. With unusual self-control, he calmed his natural reaction. Valeria marked the change and knew then that she had him.

The Greeks called it charisma. Valeria, like all women, held a piece of it within her by the happy accident of being born a girl. What followed could only be called a dance, timeless as the beginning of man and woman, Mars and Venus, endless shifting with no resolution possible, without the destruction of self.

Valeria's voice was a warm breeze across Maxentius' brow. "There was a time when you sought no counsel but mine. Name the day that changed, and I will name you the day you were betrayed by the false tongues around you! The only person you can be sure of is me."

Maxentius believed the lie in her eyes. He wanted to believe it. Valeria was not the sort of silly woman to be ignorant of her husband's natural weakness to the sorcery of her touch. Galeria trained her well to the realities of life as a noble woman. An existence whereby murder was a family disease endured without complaint, as red hair or idiocy among the children. A woman who would survive used every means at her disposal, including her body if she needed.

Valeria spoke reason to him. "Senators are but men, and you can't win their support by the mere strength of your cause. Even bribes don't ensure their loyalty. The only sure way is through their women. I am your best chance. Let me meet with the senators' wives for one afternoon, and I promise you their husbands will agree to support you. Ruricius cannot do what I can to aid this, no man can."

Valeria slid her hands across the fabric of her stola, shifting it as she went, exposing the gentle slope of her breasts in a way that was enticing and sweetly endearing at the same time.

However, Maxentius stopped her. "Ruricius is my most loyal advisor. He was present at my father's side when I was born and has served me ever since. He is my best man and my friend...you are wrong about him, wife."

Valeria retorted, "He is a low-born soldier with no mind for wartime politics. His way sees you branded a deceiver and a briber of the order of Sejanus or even Catilina, at his worst. Is that what you want? Dismiss him and raise another in his place."

"No my love, not even for you." he added a kiss to soften the blow. "But I agree with you about the Senate. Perhaps the loving touch of feminine hands will grease the wheels of fate. Have your party, but keep the guest list small. Too many and the stratagem will fail and embarrass us both. You must lean on them without falling over yourself."

Valeria chuckled when she answered him. "Yes, my lord. You want them fully convinced, I understand. Their wives will do it, have no doubt." She sat down on the couch behind her, pulling Maxentius down beside her.

"Who shall be our prey?" she mused. Her mood swung from petulance to jubilant with the ease of an indulged paramour getting her way at last. She rattled off a list of names, counting them off on her fingers. "Let's see, first of course I must invite Basilius' wife Septimia and her cousin, Flavia. She's set to marry Senator Drusus Cornelius next month. His support would be useful. Then I shall have to invite Aemilia of the Fabii and Julia Tertia, or there will be no end to the trouble...and who else?"

Maxentius kissed her forehead. "My dear, I leave all in your hands. I have other matters to attend concerning Constantine. He moves south, and we must be ready to face him."

Valeria embraced him with a sure heart. "I will not fail you, and I know you will not fail me either."

"Constantine will fall beneath my heels, I swear it, my love!"

Chapter Ten

The Wishes of Women Move Mountains

"Aarrgh!" Constantine at last gave voice to his frustrations. He sat fixed in Mediolanum, with big ideas but no sure plan to accomplish them. He sat in his study deep in thought, with only the ever faithful Aristos and Julius Asclepiodotus at his side. The desk and the floor around him were both littered with correspondence, maps, and unread scrolls from the provinces he ruled in absentia. The afternoon died away from sunshine to shades of rose and tangerine while he poured over his plans for displacing Maxentius from his perch in Rome. He discarded strategy after strategy until he could stand no more and swept his desk clean with one decisive move.

Bronze weights, a portrait of Fausta, enough vellum to choke a horse – all of it went crashing to the floor. While he stalked around the room and Julius patiently waited out the tirade, Aristos set to work making the mess disappear.

The matter at hand was a rumor of Galerius near death in the east. It was convenient news for him, but he did not yet know how to turn it into his advantage and therein lay the conundrum.

Constantine mumbled to himself as he paced. "With Galerius out of the way, I expect Maximinus

Daia and Licinius will break into open conflict in the east any day now and stop with these foolish little skirmishes. That leaves the west open for me. The only thing standing in my way is Maxentius, and he's a drunken lout in the best of times. It's almost too easy – that's what gives me pause. Julius?" he asked suddenly, catching the general off guard.

Julius startled. He was only half-listening. He took a moment to answer, buying time to collect his thoughts. "Ahem…I think you have a good point. There could be a plot afoot, there is always one afoot somewhere. Your father and I had enough defeats and setbacks to know better than to trust any of this. Maxentius knows you are no fool and he has smart men around him even if he is not. He's still very much a danger to us."

Constantine stopped in front of a bust of Pompey Magnus decorating a corner of the room. He ran his hands over the sculptured folds of the toga, admiring its form. "Yes, it is a bad sign when it doesn't seem possible to lose. The little peacock imitated what I did in Britannia to seize power in the first place, but he doesn't have a mind for warfare. With his father gone, he lacks the experience and wisdom to see this to the gory end." He kicked aside some of the fallen maps. "Damn it all, where are the routes through the Alps!" Constantine shuffled through a few of them that lay about on the floor but did not see the one he wanted.

Julius spied the map in the pile. He unfurled it on the desk for Constantine. "Here… we move the Gallic legions south of the Alps through this pass here to join us before we reach Verona. With them to add to our numbers, our chances of taking the city improve to near certainty. As word spreads of Maximian's death, confusion will also spread some desertion among Maxentius' men, I'll wager. Still, Verona will be a tough fight. The problem is that damn Ruricius Pompeianus! A better tactician is hard to find, and he will surely regroup and have another go at us."

Constantine raised an eyebrow at that.

"Present company excluded, of course," Aristo said quickly, saving face for Julius. Julius nodded his thanks to him.

Constantine laughed softly. "Maxentius could not tie his boots without Ruricius to hold the strings for him now. It would be a joke if the stakes were not so high. I intended to rid myself of a hydra's head only to see it grow back as Ruricius. Not to mention Fausta still harbors a grudge against me, as though her father's suicide were my fault."

Aristos tried and failed at tact. "Well Dominus, you did order it." He swallowed the lump that rose in his throat but it was just the truth. Constantine gave Maximian the choice of taking his own life as a noble man or dying like a criminal. Maximian chose the former and Fausta always said she understood there was no choice, but she was still devastated by it. For Aristos to say so though was rather rude.

This time Julius saved him. "He was too dangerous to live. Your wife may never agree with it – that's to be expected – but she will come to understand why it was necessary. She was the informer who told you of his plot years ago, was she not? She knew her father was untrustworthy."

"You speak truths, I can't deny it." In an

afterthought he asked, "–And where is she, my loving wife? I have not seen her since the morning meal. She made no mention of any invitations today," Constantine noted with a mildly puzzled expression. He continued studying his maps, unaware of the seriousness of his question.

Aristos and Julius exchanged looks. They both knew the Empress Fausta's whereabouts, everyone in Mediolanum knew except Constantine, but they did not dare to tell him.

"Perhaps an invitation arrived after you spoke to her. Shall I send a boy to look for her?" Aristos asked.

Constantine looked up. "Hmm? No, that's not necessary, but when she returns send her to me. I want her company tonight." He sat down behind his desk. "Enough for now. We will start again tomorrow. You're dismissed, both of you."

"As you wish, Dominus." Aristo bowed before leaving, and Julius grabbed his wine skin and made for the door, glad Constantine had not pressed further. Though Constantine said otherwise, Aristos went immediately to do something about Fausta before her husband caught her. She grew more reckless with each passing day, and the whole city whispered about Fausta and Constantine's legate Bassianus.

She had developed a noticeable habit of leaving early in the day and returning late, sometimes in different clothing and with her hair loosened where her ornatrix[20] had expertly arranged it. Her

---

[20] Slave who took care of a Roman woman's hair and make-up

disappearances went unnoticed by her husband whose war occupied most of his time. Fausta's sense of danger made her seek out men close to her husband, but Bassianus was the only fool brave enough to indulge her.

Aristos went directly to Fausta's rooms where Messalina lounged as though she were the domina. Issa sat in her lap while Messalina smoothed her coat with a jeweled brush. The pup bared her teeth, yipping at him when he approached.

"Insolent beast," he said.

Issa hopped down to growl and snap at the intruder who interrupted her grooming. Aristos shooed her away.

"You there, you know where your mistress is! The emperor is asking for her!" he barked to Messalina.

Messalina jumped to her feet. "How long has he been asking?"

"He missed her some time ago. If she does not appear soon, he will begin to ask painful questions, understand?"

Messalina nodded. Fear for herself and her mistress filled her eyes. "She's not far. Distract him, please, while I retrieve her." She grabbed her traveling cloak.

"No need, he's already distracted, but hurry. And you might want to tell her that she's becoming a little too obvious!"

Messalina nodded and disappeared from the room.

Aristo decided to wait by the front entrance so he could see for himself that Fausta arrived home. Although Aristos hated Fausta, it behooved him to keep her secrets. After a short while, the sound of Fausta's litter bearers' hurried footfalls reached him through the front door, and he knew Messalina was successful. He breathed a sigh of relief. When the empress rushed through the doorway, as expected, she was in complete disarray. Her hair was loose and wild; her cosmetics were smeared. They ran down her face like colorful wax.

"The emperor called for you, Domina," Aristo said stiffly.

If Fausta was ashamed, she did not show it. "Where is he? I would change and refresh myself first," she said. Just then, Constantine appeared in the vestibule with them.

He ran towards her, open mouthed at her appearance. "Fausta! What's happened, my love? You look as though someone set upon you in the streets! Where are your guards?"

Fausta nearly sprung from her skin in terror, but a lie found its way to her lips just as quickly. She ran to Constantine, soothing him with an elixir of sweet words and gentle caresses. "I'm well, I'm well! No cause for alarm, darling. I was caught in a sudden rain on the other side of town as I rushed home to you. I visited dear Aemilia and lost track of the hour. Messalina came to find me, to let me know you needed me."

He pulled her into his arms. "I always need you."

He leaned down to plant a kiss on her shoulder, still slick with sweat from her afternoon with Bassianus. Constantine licked his lips at the salty taste. His nose grazed her neck. Fausta was stiff with fear he could smell her lover's scent still on her, but he moved to kiss her other shoulder as well. She breaths came shallow, the risk of discovery fueled her excitement. Fausta managed to swallow it back down her throat. "And I always need you. Your devotion helps heal the wounds between us, though they are few."

He clutched at her words like a drowning man to driftwood. "So you forgive me then? You have finally come to see I had no choice about your father?"

"Before this war, before Minervina even, when your career was just beginning. Even then, my father stood between you and your plans. Now he stands no more, but there is still a debt of pain before we can truly be free of the stain. There is something that can remove it."

"Name it, and it shall be yours!"

Fausta looked up at him with big eyes. She found a few tears to aid her. "There is one thing," she said, letting them slide down her face.

She chose her next words with care. "While I visited with Aemilia, word came from her people in Nicomedia that Crispus has left the city against your orders and your mercy. What is to be done to bring this villain to justice at last? He stole my honor! He laid violent hands on me and now has fled even your generosity. What punishment for him now? My father had to kill himself, and yet the beast that bit your wife lives? You issued a Damnatio Memoriae [21]on my

---

[21] Latin phrase literally meaning "damnation of memory" - It was a form of dishonor that could be passed by the Roman Senate upon traitors or others who brought discredit to the Roman State.

father; Crispus should suffer the same. Treason is treason!"

Constantine tried to be patient with her. "The circumstances are different, Fausta. Crispus is young and foolish. He must be punished, yes, but equal with his crime and his years. Maximian started a rebellion against me and thus the state. His actions were harmful to more than just me. While Crispus' guilt is undeniable, he harmed only us."

Fausta gaped at him. "I cannot believe what I am hearing! You mean it harms only me, so what does it matter? You are Brutus to my Caesar! From one side of your mouth, you proclaim your love and fidelity, and with the other you say assaulting your wife does not matter. If my father were still alive and not dead by your hand, he would not permit me to fall to dishonor under his roof!"

Constantine seized her by the arms. "You are not under your father's roof, but mine, and do not forget it or your tongue when you speak to me. I am your emperor as well as your husband."

"Then behave like my emperor and husband. Prove you love me! Crispus tossed your mercy aside when he left Nicomedia. Why did he leave if not to raise an army to challenge you? His ambition knows no bounds; first he lays hands on me, and next he will lay them on the seat of power! What makes you so sure he will quietly fade away? He is as ambitious and determined as you!"

Constantine could not argue with her logic. "I will think on it. It is not a decision made lightly," he told her at last.

Fausta softened but a little. "That's all I ask, that you consider it and decide if your empress is worth the effort and favor you owe to her." Her smile grew mischievous. "Shall I allow a demonstration?" She wrapped her arms around him and kissed him.

Constantine tore himself away with difficulty. He smiled down at her. "You are a hellcat, woman! I should never have allowed you to pull me into your lair. Now I find it is the only place I feel at home." He laughed as he pulled her close to him. Together they headed to bed chamber.

They were barely inside the door before he tore her stola from her. The garment fell to the floor in a heap at her feet. Underneath it, she wore nothing, and her body shined with the remnants of the oil Bassianus had rubbed on her earlier as part of their passion games. Constantine stood back to look at her. She met his eyes with confidence, thrusting her chest forward so her breasts stood out to meet him. He could not help but take one into his mouth, to feel the smooth roundness of it in his hands and to tease her nipples to attention. Fausta grabbed his head while he suckled her. She ran her fingers through his hair, moaning at his touch as though she had not just done the same with Bassianus. Constantine looked up at her as she pulled his hair harder, pushing his mouth against her. When her eyes met his again, he stopped. Moving back up her body, he rummaged his fingers through her already ravaged hair and kissed her already bruised mouth.

She could taste on his lips the oil from her skin and the hint of Bassianus with it. It increased her passion, made her wild for his touch. She broke from him and headed to the bed where she laid spread out, her back arched in open invitation to him. Constantine approached her, a wicked smile on his face, before he buried it between her thighs. Fausta moaned and squirmed with pleasure but before his tongue could find its favorite places, or perhaps traces of Bassianus, she pulled his head up and into her face. Kissing him deeply, she let her hand trail down his back, along his waist and then lower, on a mission to please both of them. Finding him hard and ready, she slid him inside her, experiencing with him the explosion of two souls connecting in the cosmos.

Fausta clutched his body to hers and her moans were the sound of waves crashing against an unforgiving shore and the lovers rode them together. Later, when they came back to reality, his face was above hers, staring down at her, watching her intently as they drowned and were reborn together. He locked his lips on hers briefly, then flipped her over with ungentle hands. He surprised her and her first gasp was not pleasure but in unexpected, though short-lived pain.

The time for softness and romance had passed, now they were on to something less sweet but more fun. Gripping her waist, he took her in a brutal way that required the trust between them be intact. It heightened the experience of physical love through marriage, giving focus and clarity to their passions.

They rode higher and faster and changed position yet again. She clutched his hips and matched his pace. They moved together, faster then slower, now deeper, now harder. They raced towards a beautiful conclusion. Fausta moved her hands from his hips to his back and held him tight to her. When he was close to finishing, and she knew it, she locked her legs around him tightly, pulling him to her so that he could not escape to spill his seed anywhere but inside her. They screamed together and finished together, and it was a glorious end.

Later, they lay in the bed, completely spent. They had enjoyed each other for hours. She turned to him, wrapped in the twisted bedcovers. Her hair lay across the pillow beside her; her face was flushed and her lips still full and red as a pomegranate.

She raised herself on her arms. "I wish that we could stay here forever just like this. How would it be if the world outside these doors could vanish and leave you to enjoy your greatest prize whenever you wished?"

Constantine snuggled his head into her neck where mounds of soft hair enveloped him in the calming scents of almonds and cherry blossoms. He breathed deep of her. "That would suit me above all things. Let us make it so – no more war and conquest. You conquered the conqueror." He whispered it against her neck; the sound tickled her and vibrated all the way down her back from the way she shivered under his touch.

"You tease me when you know I would give anything to see it so."

"Would you?" His interest piqued. "You would see me conquered? You seek to accomplish what your brother and father could not?"

"Conquered only in that the wishes of your heart would lead you no further than my arms, and this stupid war finished and behind us. I wonder that you are working toward that or do you fight just to do so?" She studied her husband for a moment before she decided something. "I will know of what's coming for me." Fausta sat up to clap her hands for Messalina.

She materialized on command, standing in the doorway, as much a goddess as Fausta and at her lady's command.

"See that none disturb us for the remainder of the night," Fausta ordered. She turned to her husband. "And as for you…show me you trust me, as I trusted you. I told you about my father's plans, stayed by your side when you destroyed him. If you intend to keep killing my family members, I think it's the least you can do." Fausta let her brow furrow with playful anger she knew thrilled her husband.

When Messalina left to instruct the guards, Constantine rolled over to rest against the pillows, deep in thought and still basking in the afterglow of their lovemaking. It inspired closeness within him that might have been missing had she pressed him on his plans any other time or place.

"You're right, my love. That is the least but not all I can do. Soon this war will be over and I shall have my empire and my empress by my side until I die. My word and my will shall govern the empire for generations to come through my sons and grandsons. Through you," here he stopped to clasp protectively a section of her thigh, pliant and smooth and soft as cheese under his fingers, "I will have many sons to carry my family name into the next millennium."

Fausta's giggle was high, clear and rang musical to him. "How can you be so sure you will emerge the victor? Please be careful, my love. I could not bear to lose you. My brother's legions still outnumber yours and more importantly, he holds Rome."

"Rome is but the cradle that rocks him and his men do not know real battle. My men have been fighting Germans, Picts and all manner of savages. Maxentius' lazy homegrown rebels do not trouble me.

Fausta interrupted him, saying, "Rome is more than a cradle. The city has declined over the years, that's true enough, but the man who rules Rome rules the empire."

Constantine lifted himself higher on the pillows. "Just whose side are you on?" he said, only half joking.

Fausta made a coquettish face at him. She simpered, "you ask what you already know. I say it only to help you uncover any obstacles in your way."

Constantine roared with laughter. "So you are the general now my dear? Which strategy do you wish me to employ? I live to serve you!" His hands moved to encircle her waist, but Fausta slapped them away.

"Stop laughing, you silly man! Wars have been won on the strength of a woman's counsel before now. The gods have always used us to guide men down the right paths."

"The gods? I'll leave them to you and you leave the war planning to me. My men even now move south to invade Italy. I'll descend upon Rome as a savior spreading wrath to her enemies. The people will love me!"

"At present, the people belong to my brother, my dear. I have heard from the slaves that even the Christians are being shown some measure of favor. Maxentius has endorsed their selection of a bishop and let him take office, and he stopped the most outrageous of the property seizures. Every good Roman is applauding his mercy."

"They applaud him now, but when their bellies grow empty, they will curse him again. He cannot feed them!" Constantine said without explaining his meaning.

When Fausta asked him, he refused to say. He turned the conversation back to his war plans.

Fausta shared his enthusiasm for the subject. "So you will march south, gathering support from peasants as you go; what stops Maxentius from doing the same with his men to block your way?"

"He has only a vague idea at the most. Your brother is quite stupid, my dear. We need only strike hard and fast and all Italia will yield to our cause. We will create an unstoppable river of blood, enough to drown Maxentius in its wake. With Rome and the West under my control, I will only have the east left to conquer before my position is beyond question."

Constantine's voice rose as his excitement grew, a fire lit his eyes. In them, lay the passion of his conviction as bare as they had been when he had taken her mere hours ago. Fausta mirrored his passions and his ambitions. "And who shall stand beside you when you are the emperor of the entire world?" she said, rising to her knees beside him. She pulled him up with her.

Constantine smiled at her. "My loving wife, of course. Who else?" His kiss was gentle on her lips.

Still kneeling beside her, he went on, speaking the words into her ear, a lover's whisper. "Our time is coming, my dove. The people of Italy are a fickle lot. I expect many of them are tired of the fighting and will surrender without bloodshed."

Fausta sank down beside him, her shoulders slumped. "They are not alone in this. Seeing our families at odds has weighed on me these last six years. And worse, I see no end in sight. When the

West is won, you'll set your sights eastward. When does it end?"

"It ends, my dear, when the full empire is in the safe hands my father planned. Don't fret; trouble in the East is a distant thought. For the time being, Licinius holds it as an ally, and he keeps Maximinus Daia at bay, ever the trapped rabbit. Until that changes, I will focus my attentions where they are most needed – on Maxentius and mother Rome."

"So everything hinges on what happens in the East, both for your son and for your allies. And tell me love; what happens when fighting in the East is not just a distant thought? Will you turn on your allies to secure power and at the same time, leave a traitor to nestle at your breast? When…"

Constantine covered Fausta's mouth with his, silencing her. "Enough politics – I would rather nestle at your breast," he murmured. His hands roamed over her body again. Any further questions about his motives or plans would have to wait, she thought, as she succumbed to his reignited passion.

Later they lay together, each in their own quiet places of deep thought. Constantine's thoughts were concentrated on his future plans and Fausta on hers. Unbeknownst to her husband, Messalina had charted her menses yesterday and declared Fausta was entering the moon phase when she was most fertile. Fausta's meeting with Bassianus had not happened on a whim, but rather was a calculated step to secure what the house of Constantius needed most, a male heir to establish the dynasty. Between husband and lover, she was sure to produce a son this time.

"Paestum! Why on earth should I go there?" Fausta shouted the next morning, shattering the bliss that had enveloped them since last night. It was early morning, and Fausta had been lying in bed watching as Aristos dressed Constantine for the day ahead, as he had also dressed his father. She had become entranced watching the steady hands of the old slave as he ran them over Constantine's under-tunic, smoothing it for his armor. Her thoughts led her to imagine that Constantine was just a man and she just the woman who loved him. That it could be that simple was the basic truth that was nonetheless an amazing lie as well for such singular persons.

Constantine reminded her of their special roles in life when he announced she was to depart for Paestum immediately. "Because I have commanded it! No hand shall stand idle in this conflict. You will go to your father's villa there, stopping along the way to curry support from his friends and clients in Italy. It's your duty to aid where and when you are able."

The last traces of satisfaction left Fausta's face, replaced by indignant anger. "How will it appear to have your wife soliciting your enemies on your behalf? I will not go!"

Constantine was firm. "You will go, because they aren't my enemies; but your friends, and still hold your family in high regard. Your father's villa belongs to you now. It is perfectly reasonable that you should examine the condition of his holdings. You will throw lavish parties; tell everyone all is well in our camp. Entice others to join their fortunes to me, to us."

Fausta took a gamble, telling him. "You speak the truth when you say 'us.' And that is the only way I will do it, if it is for us. You will not parade me as a trophy without something in it for me. Condemn Crispus and promise elevation for my children as your legitimate heirs, and I will do all you say and more."

Constantine was surprised at her persistence. "That you would continue to press when we have already discussed, he must have wounded you much deeper than I thought, but do not press me further. I said I would think about it, and I will." His reply ended the argument.

"As you say – I will tell my ladies to prepare." Fausta groused as Messalina walked into the room holding Fausta's robes, just warmed in the morning fire. She held them out as Fausta slipped into them, enjoying the robe and the comfort of Messalina's arms around her.

"You heard the emperor's command?" Fausta asked her.

"Yes, Domina. I have already spoken to the staff. Preparations are underway. We will be ready to leave by mid-day meal. I thought you might need more comfort this morning, so I warmed your robe, and your favorite morning meal is waiting for you in the triclinium."

Fausta sighed. "What would I do without you, Messalina?"

Chapter Eleven

Murder in Cappadocia

"I'm not a little girl you need to protect!" Julia finally shouted in utter frustration.

For two weeks, Crispus, Licinius and the rest of the men had been treating her as though she was a fragile ornament since they left Nicomedia. They meant well, but she had enough of it. Bandits watching them from the shadows as they passed by would never have believed they were men simply traveling together. They rode in a circle around her, more like bodyguards than fellow riders. Someone was always rushing to help her dismount her horse or stand guard near her when she walked a few paces into the forests to relieve herself.

The men discussed the problem among themselves when they thought she was asleep. Lying in her tent, Julia heard everything, and none of it was good.

"She shouldn't have come. It's slowing us down and making a hard road harder!" Licinius groused one night as the men tried to find comfortable sleeping spots outside while Julia rested safe, warm and alone inside the only tent.

The others murmured agreements, and even the usually reserved Donatus offered an opinion.

"She does not wish it to be so. She is as frustrated as we are. Perhaps if Crispus spoke to her, she would allow us to send her back."

"Donatus is right. You should talk to her," Licinius said to Crispus. "Convince her she made a terrible mistake. She'll get one of us killed before this is over. Mark me, it will come to that!"

Crispus came to her defense, she noticed, but as always, he gave with one hand and took back with the other. "Let's not talk about this as though we are actually thinking about doing it! She will never let us send her back before she wants to go. We'll just have to wait until we reach Cappadocia. We'll try to send her home from there, or more likely, she'll be ready to leave by then."

As Julia lay in her tent, listening to them, she wanted so much to defend herself. She wanted to tell them what she thought of their grand plot, but a small part of her wondered if they were right. For the past few days, she had been debating if she should give in to the men's doubt and grumbles. Part of her longed to tell Crispus she wanted to go home, but even as she thought the hateful words, her spirit rejected them. It was not in her to accept defeat. Instead, she searched for some way to settle the issue on her own. A means soon presented itself in the most unexpected way.

It happened as they entered the wilderness of Cappadocia where the barren rock landscape formed beautiful structures that were some of the most fantastical shapes in the natural world. The party of friends reached the sparse, high plains at mid-day when the view was spectacular. As far as they could see, there was only pale rock, so soft it rubbed off on the skin like arsenic powder on the cheeks. The water and weather had battered the landscape into tall, cone-shaped towers, mushroom domes, and layers of rock that resembled goose feathers laid out on top of each other.

In between the cliffs lay random meadows, flowing streams here and there with pale flowering bushes and evergreens. Dotted along the hillside, and through the rock clusters, ran a honeycomb network of tunnels and dwellings cut from the soft formations. The manmade tunnels were centuries old, and new ones appeared the further the party traveled into the heart of the country. Cappadocia had always been a mystical place. The mere mention of the name brought to mind a glorious wasteland where only the hardiest of people lived; in beauty only a god could have created.

There was one saving grace for them in the wilderness, courtesy of Lactantius, from his days wandering in the East. He gave Crispus the name of a high official who could help them. Basil of Cappadocia was a scholar, a rhetorician, and a devoted Christian alongside his wife, Emmelia. Despite the group being strangers to him, Crispus held hope that Lactantius' stories about him were true. They would never make it across the vast wasteland without friends and shelter along the way.

Everyone was tired, dusty and frustrated, but Crispus did not plan to call a halt until they neared an area where the map showed an oasis. Getting there proved difficult. One hour turned into three, and still they wandered. With so barren a landscape, it was easy to become confused in the sun's unyielding glare. Their progress was slow. Slow and methodical enough that everyone except Julia failed to sense the trouble lurking on their heels. She tried to tell the men but all of them dismissed her fears. Nonetheless, all day she was plagued by a general unease. She constantly searched the horizon and stopped short many times to listen. Her efforts produced nothing.

And yet there was a cause for her worry. Crispus and his friends were not the only travelers making for the oasis. The mercenaries led by Charietto had arrived the previous day and camped close by it.

Just before sunset, the lake and surrounding trees of the oasis came into view. Finally, Crispus called an exhausted halt to the day's ride. The men dropped like stones from their horses. With the last of their strength, they made ready the campsite and Julia prepared an evening meal of warm porridge and dried fruit. As they ate, Julia suddenly stopped eating mid-bite. She heard strange sounds. Whispered voices that carried on the twilight breeze. She told the men, but again they dismissed her. Annoyed, Julia walked a few paces away then thought better of it. She returned to her horse to retrieve her bow and quiver of arrows.

"I'm going to have a look around," she declared. "I heard something even if none of you believe it."

Before anyone could rise to stop her or offer much protest, Julia disappeared into the trees behind them. Crispus surveyed their surroundings. Finding no cause for alarm, he shrugged and returned to his porridge.

"No doubt she'll soon return empty-handed. She might be a good bowman, but there's naught here but snakes and ticks!"

Julia paid no attention to him. She ventured further into the trees. She was getting close to something, or it was getting close to her; either way she was glad she had a weapon. *Whatever, whoever is stalking us, please let me see it first,* she prayed silently.

Around her, the twilight deepened until she was alone in near darkness save the light of the half moon. Moving soundlessly, she did her best to disguise her presence.

After a short while, she reached an area where the trees formed a dark heart in the wilderness. Within the circle of trees, there were at least a dozen men, large and Germanic in look and dress. Some stood whispering in small groups; others sharpened weapons, and still others were just beginning to rouse themselves from sleep. While she hid, she listened to their plans to attack when the moon was high. She heard one of them say Crispus' name and even more terrifying, her own name.

Julia froze, but there was no need. The strangers had not noticed her approach, and she did not linger. She crouched down, scrambling on hands and knees until she was clear of them. She beat a fast retreat to the campsite where the others were looking around for her, concern on their faces. When they saw her coming; their concern turned to anger. Crispus already had his mouth open to berate her. Breathless and agitated, she had to swallow several gulps of water before she could speak of what she had seen. After several false starts on her part, the men at last began to understand.

"Father have mercy upon us!" Donatus prayed.

Julia was more practical. "We are badly outnumbered. I counted at least twelve of them, maybe more. We should break camp and hide among the rocks until daybreak. Perhaps they will think we fled in the night and give chase. We can slip away behind them."

Licinius was defiant. "And if they realize the game and chase us down? I say we make our stand now! Let them come – I will not die like a dog chased into the wild!"

"How much time do we have?" Crispus asked Julia. He peered into the distance, in the direction from which she returned to them.

"An hour at the most. They were still rising from sleep when I saw them. I heard a few words of their conversation as I fled. They mean to attack us when the moon is at the zenith."

Crispus was quiet, thinking. The others waited for him to decide their plan of action. There was only one, he decided, telling them, "Our best hope is to attack first. If they can use darkness, so can we."

"My thoughts exactly!" Licinius agreed.

Crispus went on, "There's no time to waste. We must catch them before they can come at us with their full strength. Their numbers won't count if we can surprise them and kill a few off quickly." As risky as his plan was, no one spoke against it.

They all followed Julia back to the clearing where the enemy was camped. Crouching below the line of sight, the men prepared to rush forward. Charietto and his men were oblivious, they sat around a small pile of glowing embers, talking quietly among themselves as they waited for to strike. Julia slid back from the others to take up a place behind one of the trees. Placing her bow into position, she loaded an arrow and prepared to fire.

"Good," Crispus whispered. "Julia can watch from the shadows and pick off any that escape us when the fighting begins."

"Let us remind these fools why Romans are so feared!" Licinius said. He and Crispus touched their blades together, pride swelling in their chests. Silently they closed in on the camp. The night favored them. The moon disappeared behind some clouds, leaving the sky as inky black as night seas. Heavy streams of fog had rolled in from the lake, weaving past their feet. It moistened the ground and hid their footfalls. Licinius took the point position to Crispus' right. Donatus took the left, Quintus moved to the back to serve as a rear defense.

Two guards, unseen until were guarding the perimeter but were deep in a debate on the various attributes of Persian prostitutes. It was no trouble for Crispus and Licinius to approach on cat feet, seize them from behind and cut their throats before they could sound an alarm.

Crispus waved to signal the way was clear. He and Licinius exchanged a nod and on a count of three, they rushed into the camp, swords slashing murderously at Charietto's unprepared men. Quintus and Donatus raced in behind them with equally lethal intent, falling upon their enemy without mercy.

The men slashed and stabbed while Julia methodically picked off two or three with well-aimed arrows to the heart and head. Crispus had her to thank for his life when she managed to shoot through the eye a tall, muscular brute who knocked away Crispus' sword and was swinging killing blows at him. Crispus dodged them, but barely. Julia's shot was a gale of wind that jolted the mercenary off his feet. The man's screams might have been endless had Crispus not thrust his reclaimed sword deep into the man's chest, silencing him. Licinius raised a loud, triumphant whoop and redoubled his efforts against his own man. In short order, another of Charietto's men lay dead.

The scales tipped in their favor as the entire gang was slaughtered until only Charietto himself remained alive. He backed away from them, armed with two daggers that he welded double-handed. Desperation and fear belied his confident taunts at them.

"Come for me...if you have the nerve," Charietto shouted at them. Standing with his blades drawn he was a cobra ready to strike dead the first person who moved on him.

Crispus and Licinius let their training and their skills speak for them. Crispus, Donatus and Quintus approached from the front of him, while Licinius moved around to his side. Charietto saw it happening, watched everything from the corner of his eye but was powerless to do anything save growl, crouch lower to spring and clutch his daggers tighter. His feet bounced slightly as he readied himself for their assault. Crispus took the lead. He struck with precision, aiming at Charietto's head.

Charietto dodged the blow and returned it. Crispus anticipated his swing. He blocked it with the edge of his sword. Licinius rushed forward from the side in his own assault and he and Crispus took turns engaging him.

While Charietto was distracted with them, Donatus managed to get behind him and stab him in the shoulder, disabling an arm. Charietto growled in pain and his blade fell from a hand unable to hold it. Exploited the hole in the ring they formed around him, he raced to a nearby tree. Wounded yet more dangerous than ever, he backed up against it, panting and sneering at them.

Charietto was steeling himself for his final stand when Julia pinned him to the tree with a shot through the injured shoulder that made him howl worse than a tortured dog but did not kill him, yet. Spouting more curses at them, he tried in vain to put the bolt out, then lay back against the tree in defeat. He wiped his hands, slick with his own blood, across his forehead leaving it smeared, a sacrifice anointed for death. Crispus came to stand in front of him.

"Tell me who sent you, or I will make you hurt much worse than you are now," he told him and meant it. When Charietto hesitated, Crispus took it as an insult. He twisted the bolt further into Charietto's body. Charietto gasped in pain but to his credit, did not call out again.

He spit blood from his mouth. "Brought down by a damn stick of wood – after all this time, I expected better. Who wields it?"

Julia emerged from the shadows in triumph. "I did it. I shot you, you bastard!"

Charietto saw her and managed a weak laugh which became a moan, "I always knew it would be a woman who got me in the end." He turned to Crispus. "I need no help dying. The information is yours for the asking. I want you to know you're a dead man too. Emperor Maxentius hunts you, boy. He wants you gone before your father can take you back and he will send others to finish what I've started. Every free man in the empire will be looking to collect the bounty on your head, so do your worst to me. I'll see you in the afterlife."

Charietto's lips curled as he ranted at them. He spit at Crispus and gave a satisfied grunt to see the spittle spray across Crispus' face. Crispus jumped back in surprise. He wiped the spittle away, enraged.

"You first!" he roared, driving his dagger into Charietto's chest. Charietto's eyes grew wide; he gasped then went still. His head lolled and dropped down on his shoulders.

All around them lay the bodies of Charietto's men. His intended victims were unscathed mostly, except Donatus, who took a dagger to the thigh at some point in the melee. Julia cut the clothing off one of the dead men to make a tight bandage for him until they could get him back to camp and properly stitch his wound.

Crispus looked around at the campsite they now controlled. "Take everything of value. We'll stack the bodies and then burn them. Tomorrow we make for Caesarea Mazaca and the safety of old friends."

"Are you sure we will find a welcome there?" Licinius asked. "Maybe we should take what these men have and bypass the city."

Crispus disagreed with him. "It's not enough to carry us to Helena. We must stop and fully replenish our supplies. The fates are with us, they won't see us abandoned."

Donatus spoke up with a grimace of pain

while Julia put pressure on his wound to slow the bleeding. "It was not the fates which saved us today. God favors our cause for the sake of His son." He looked around at them as though pleading with them to agree with him.

Licinius was the first to scoff at his claim. "God? It was Julia finding her mark so well that made the difference tonight." He turned to her. "I was wrong about you. I'm sorry I ever doubted you. You're as skilled as any warrior I have seen. Speed and accuracy are qualities we need. I'm glad you're with us."

Crispus echoed him with his own praise. "He's right. We owe you our respect...and I owe you my life."

"I would have your respect – and nothing more. I only did what any of you would have done," she told him and went back to her task with renewed determination and vigor now that she was proven an asset rather than a burden.

194

Chapter Twelve

The Kindness of Strangers

Newly supplied with the food and gear from Charietto and his desperados, Crispus and his friends were able to reach Caesarea Mazaca in only two days' time. They arrived just as dawn was breaking over the foothills that surrounded the fire mountain Argaeus. They reached the agora situated at edge of the Caesarea first. Slaves and tradesmen scurried about, throwing open shop doors and windows, setting up booths and placing goods on tables in the marketplace. The friends marveled as they ventured between the various shops, carved ingeniously from solid rock in shades of pink, red and brown.

Despite the beauty around him, Licinius was the first to lose interest in the sights of Caesarea. His belly growled loudly, revealing what he wanted most.

"Ugh," he moaned. "I hope Basil will offer a morning meal. I should not have drunk so much wine. I'll die of a pounding head if I don't eat soon."

Julia laughed at him. "That's what comes of being a sot[22]! The rest of us aren't complaining, but we were not so silly as to drink an entire wineskin at

---

[22] A drunkard

once either. You deserve nothing less so don't complain now!"

Licinius rubbed his temples. "Well, the wine was excellent. I say it was worth it. Who would have imagined hired killers would carry such a delicious Alban on them? They probably murdered someone to get it and their loss is my gain."

"Well then – suffer the consequences of your 'gain' in silence," Crispus said, rather sharper than he intended.

Licinius looked at him in surprise. "Why the vitriol so early in the day, cousin? A black mood makes for a bad start of it."

Crispus' grimness went unabated by Licinius' bantering. "Is foolery going to keep us alive? If Basil turns us away, we will be without means to reach Armenia. Perhaps you should turn your thoughts to that instead."

He did not know why he was annoyed, except that it was sometimes lonely being the one everyone else depended upon to keep them alive. The last thing Crispus wanted was to lead his friends into a wilderness to die, and he had no guarantee that was not exactly what he had done. He risked own life many times, on the battlefield and in situations brought on by ignorance or plain stupidity. It was quite another to lead his friends into a same sticky mess. The thought weighed heavily on him that morning while they crossed into Caesarea and it made him poor company. He groused, grumbled and snapped at anyone who asked him anything at all.

Finally, Licinius begged for mercy. "Stop it, cousin!" He said, holding out his hands. "Basil will heed our petitions, and if he doesn't, you'll convince him otherwise…you always do."

"I'm glad you're so confident. Of course, I would be too if I had the luxury of letting someone else make the decisions," Crispus grumbled. "There is nothing for you to do this morning except nurse your aching head. If you have no suggestions to help, then at least spare me your false encouragement. I haven't the stomach for it."

With that, he nudged Viatoro and moved ahead of the group to ride alone. Julia made to ride after him, but Licinius stopped her.

"You will be no better received than I was. Leave him alone for a bit. He'll be fine. The other night was a close call; he's understandably feeling out of sorts about it. What if you hadn't been there?"

Julia looked into the near distance after Crispus. "But I was – that's the important part. We're all in this together!"

"He knows that. So you don't need to tell him again. Come on, let us hear again how you picked them off one by one," Licinius said, changing to a subject on which Julia would be happy to indulge him.

Crispus need not have worried about the reception Basil would give them. They appeared to him dirty from the road and weary from all that had happened to them. Basil was surprised at the arrival of the three bedraggled nobles and their guards at his door, but he was gracious in his welcome once Crispus spoke of Lactantius.

Basil was a middle-aged man; streaks of gray ran through his black hair, but there was power in his step. He was broad-shouldered and tall with a bearing that spoke of a man used to giving orders and seeing them followed.

He led them into his rock-hewn home where beautiful wall tapestries made up for the lack of natural light. The speckled granite floors tiles radiated heat from a buried hypocaust system[23]. The furniture was made of lightweight wood. Simple, sturdy pieces built for comfort rather than appearance. The only finery was in the religious ornaments scattered about; delicate crosses, and brightly-colored paintings depicting Christ with his twelve apostles.

Basil ordered his servants to see to their comfort, offering them fresh bread, boiled eggs, cheese and goat's milk for refreshment. Licinius behaved as a starving waif. He sat down and grabbed a section of bread and an egg. He stuffed them into his mouth before anyone else could say a word and without any embarrassment. Julia for one was mortified for all of them. She would have apologized for her crude companion, but that would have just brought more attention to the lack of breeding Licinius displayed.

Basil and his wife Emmelia met with them in his triclinium. His wife said little to them, leaving the conversation to her husband. She was a petite woman, years his junior, with a kind if not pretty face and brown hair she wore in a chignon at the nape of her neck.

When they were all comfortably settled with food and drink, Basil queried the group. "It has been many years since Lactantius and I saw each other.

---

[23] A Roman system of indoor heating by the use of furnaces that piped hot air through the house via tubes in the floors and walls, usually found only in wealthy homes

How does he fare? Any friend of his is mine as well." Basil's wide smile was engaging and sincere.

Julia made small talk with her hosts exclaiming, "Your home is lovely! Especially the memorial to your family." She pointed to an alcove behind Basil. It was decorated by honeycombed holes cut into the stone. Each niche held the wax mask of an ancestor, mimicking the Roman custom of displaying them in the vestibule of the house. In the very center of it sat a large bronze and bejeweled cross, intricately wrought and occupying a place of high honor.

"Yes, it is beautiful. You have a good eye," Basil told her. "Tell me something truthfully? Have you brought danger to my house today? I have a right to know why I'm offering sanctuary."

"I have no intention to bring harm to you or your family, sir. I can assure you of that." Crispus said, taking care to keep his tone mild. "I can offer you my support and fidelity when this is over, if you will give me yours now. I swear you and your family are safe, but I don't wish to lie to you about how I came to be in Cappadocia."

Crispus took a deep steadying breath. "My father the Augustus Constantine, banished me to Nicomedia for crimes against the state, sir. I was not supposed to leave, and to give me aid is punishable as treason, but my father greatly respects Christians. He will not harm one who helped me, and to my knowledge he doesn't yet know I'm not in Nicomedia. I left to seek out my grandmother who is in great danger in Armenia. I take a change revealing this to you. You could turn me over to my father, but Lactantius trusts you and I trust his judgment."

Basil's brow furrowed. "What was the crime that caused your father to turn against you?"

Crispus gave him the truth. "I am accused of raping the Empress Fausta, my stepmother."

Emmelia drew a sharp breath at the news. Julia shifted her chair to sit closer to her. She whispered an explanation to calm her as only another woman could do. The assembly of men was not privy to what Julia said to her, but Emmelia's expression changed from shocked anger to acceptance, and she held her peace.

"A terrible accusation! If you are innocent, there must be more to the story, or your father would not have given it credence," Basil inquired.

It was the question they feared. Crispus waited a moment before answering. To lie to a man like Basil was a terrible thing he had just promised not to do.

And yet he did. "No, sir. There is no more to the story than that my stepmother has bewitched him and plots against me. I am innocent." His friends' lives were at stake, he decided, and it was the truth, for the most part.

"And?" Basil persisted.

"And I need refuge. My friends and I were ambushed." He pointed to Donatus, who along with Quintus sat slightly apart from the others. His reddish brown skin had taken on a grayish hue. He held his hand over his wound, which needed the dressing changed. Donatus could not have looked more sickly.

"My man here has a wound which will fester if not properly attended. He needs rest but we cannot stay here long. We must reach Armenia – my grandmother needs me!"

Basil held up a hand. "A dilemma to be sure." He waved a servant towards Donatus. "Of course we will tend to your man's wounds." The servant led a grateful Donatus away into the recesses of the house. "But beyond that…do you understand my problem? I must consider my family. To risk my lovely Emmelia…" He gestured to his wife with a look of tenderness. "…and my mother? And for what cause, so that I may harbor the emperor's wayward son accused of a rape? "

Basil stopped talking. He waited for Crispus to answer his charge. In the interim, a dignified elderly woman entered the room. She sat down quietly beside Emmelia. While everyone watched, the two women began whispering to each other, their heads close together. They appeared to debate something between them until, with a gentle touch on the arm, the older woman silenced the younger one. She rose from her seat with some effort. Basil turned his full attention to her and so did the others.

"My mother, the lady Macrina," he announced to the room at large with a proud smile.

Macrina had been Basil's closest ally since his father's passing some years prior. Despite her advanced age, she was still a comely woman. She was formidable, her bearing all the more imposing beside Emmelia, who simpered mouse-like as her mother-in-law spoke with an authority beyond her age and gender.

"Basil, they must be given refuge," she decided, leaving no room for further arguments. "Our Christian duty commands us to do no less. If we fall as a result, we shall meet Christ in heaven as our reward."

Basil acquiesced. "As you say, mother…it is our duty."

Emmelia nodded her assent as well. "Come with me, all of you. I will see you to rooms." She stood for them to follow her.

She spoke to them along the way. "No one in this house will reveal your presence here," she told them. "Nonetheless, do not overly engage the servants. Their tongues are not as mute as ours."

She led the group through a labyrinth of rooms and halls the likes of which they had not seen before. The house was built in the style of a Roman villa but with noticeable differences. The various rooms were carved from the rock and dimly lit. The floors gradually sloped downward as they headed deeper into the house. In the place of windows and a compluvium[24], the elaborate wall hangings continued through the entire house, and the ceilings were covered in tile mosaics. In all manner of vivid colors, the mosaics shimmered in the light of the many flaming braziers placed throughout the house. As they all took in the scene around them, Emmelia explained how she and her family came to be in Cappadocia themselves.

"This family has been of means for many generations – our wealth and good name kept us safe when Galerius and Diocletian's murderous edicts were causing the slaughter of many of our dear friends and acquaintances. I too was born into a prosperous family. I came to my marriage with a heavy dowry and with our wealth and influence, we

---

[24] The open space above the atrium in Roman homes through which rain water was collected for household use.

helped as many as we could until accused of sedition ourselves. We suffered grievous losses of family and a great deal of our wealth, now replenished. My husband's father died a martyr when he refused to bow before a statue of Augustus Divine. Forgive our hesitation, born of a remembrance of our worst days. Macrina is right. We must always help others if we can." She stopped outside a series of doors. "And here are your rooms. I hope you find them comfortable."

"Thank you, Madame. We are grateful for whatever house room your family grants us." Crispus said.

The small rooms were located across from each other. A little further down the hall was another room where Emmelia directed Quintus to join Donatus, who already resting inside. He offered his own expressions of gratitude.

"A private room for us? What luxury! We never expected to be shown such courtesy!" he exclaimed, having expected he and Donatus would bed down with the servants.

While Quintus joined Donatus, Julia peeked inside one room while Crispus and Licinius went into the other. It did not take very long; there was not much to see, actually. The rooms sat bare of adornment save an iron cross on the mantle above the fireplace. There was a worn dressing table and a backless chair that looked almost as uncomfortable as the small bed with its thin, well-worn mattress. Emmelia smiled as she gestured inside the room and stated the obvious. "We live very simply here."

Julia followed Emmelia inside. She smiled brightly. "After so many nights sleeping in a tent, I would like nothing better than to feel a bed beneath me again. A long, restful sleep is just what I need!"

Across the hallway, Crispus and Licinius could be heard arguing about their sleeping arrangements. The debated became a ribald session of insults, and Licinius aimed a particularly ugly curse at his cousin.

"Pedicabo ego vos et irrumabo[25]!" he said with a loud guffaw.

Emmelia blanched.

Julia turned bright pink with embarrassment. "Excuse their squabbling. Men are no better than children when it comes to sharing."

Emmelia managed a nervous laugh. "Indeed! But though I take no offense, I would ask you to caution them against their rough language in the presence of my mother-in-law." With a short nod, she disappeared down the hallway, clucking her tongue as she passed by the men's room.

Julia raced across the hallway. "You two are incorrigible! How can you speak like that, knowing full well the lady of the house is right next door? Does this look like a bawdy house to you? Shameless!"

Licinius was his usual self. "Actually it does, and a cheap one at that." He laughed and plopped down on the bed he and Crispus had been fighting over. There was only one in the room; the other piece of furniture was a wooden bench with a few pillows tossed across it.

"Well, that's no excuse for acting like fools! We are lucky they took us in and even luckier she

---

[25] From Catullus, Latin phase meaning to anally and orally rape someone.

didn't throw us out just now!"

"We didn't know she could hear us. We thought she was with you!" Licinius protested.

"Calm down, Julia," Crispus said. "It was an honest mistake. We didn't realize how loud we were – we're just glad to have reached safety. I'll speak to Emmelia later to offer my apologies."

Julia was unappeased. "The dead could have heard you! Must I serve as mother to you both?"

Licinius gave her a mischievous look. "Can we nurse from you as well since you're to be our mother?" In a flash, Julia gave him a semi-playful slap across the face. Unbothered, Licinius grabbed the offending hand.

"And now you beat me too? Well, I won't have it. You stay here with your other 'child' if you want. I'm taking the other room. You two can share a bed. You know you've wanted to since we left Nicomedia!" With that, he strode from the room and into Julia's room next door. As he passed Crispus, he gave him a helpful grin Julia thankfully did not see.

Standing in his wake though, Julia was appalled. "Does he really mean to take my room from me?" she asked, astonished at his nerve. The sound of the lock turning in place gave her answer. Julia made for the locked door to protest, but Crispus stopped her.

With a good-natured shrug, he said, "Is it really so horrible to share a room with me? We slept in the same bed at times when we were children. Why not now?"

He wrapped an arm around Julia's waist, spinning her towards him in a playful manner. Their faces were only inches apart, and Julia turned bright pink for the second time that day. She pushed away from him, unnerved by his touch.

"As I recall, you never played fair, and you still don't. I should leave you on that bench or worse in the hallway to share space with the mice," she said, trying and failing to regain her composure.

"But you won't." Crispus laughed at her consternation. "I'm going to get some rest. Join me if you like…or not. Your choice."

With no further ado, Crispus took off his boots and collapsed onto the bed fully dressed. In short order, he was snoring, but too loudly to be genuine. Julia weighed her options. She could risk alarming her host by pounding on the door for Licinius to get out, or she could get into the bed with Crispus.

"Between Scylla and Charybdis[26]…" She took a deep, steadying breath and made her decision. She climbed into the bed with Crispus.

"Do not think this pleases me," she said to his back. He shifted a bit but said nothing. "You keep to your side, and I will keep on mine."

Over his shoulder, he mumbled, "You need not worry."

Julia was glad his back was to her. He did not see her grimace at his rebuke. As she lay beside him, nervous tension, and the excitement of being so close to him gave way to a bone-deep weariness that swallowed her whole, and she joined Crispus in a deep and exhausted sleep.

---

[26] Mythical sea monsters that threatened from each side of a narrow strait; meaning a choice between two equally hazardous situations

Hours later, a hard knock at the door disturbed the cocoon of peaceful sleep that enveloped them. Startled, Crispus bolted upright from his prone position, shoving aside Julia's arms and legs from where they had roamed across him while she slept.

The door to the room crept open as a small man, not much taller than the door handle, appeared carrying a large tray of food and an amphora of wine. "I'm sorry to disturb you. The domina sends refreshments," he said with a smile. "She had supplies for the missus I am to deliver as well. I thought her room was next door, but I see she sleepwalked into your bed. Shall I leave them here instead?" He asked with a look of feigned innocence.

Julia was still groggy and inclined to ignore the impertinent suggestion. She turned her back on the man while Crispus laughed at the servant's cheekiness. Then he served him some of his own. "What is your name, little man? That tray is bigger than you are."

"Petronius, sir. I was a free man once, and I suppose it sometimes shows. Don't tell the domina, or she'll have me punished." Despite his small stature, he moved about the room with grace and agility that belied his physical limitations.

"No worry on that, I'm joking with you. How long have we slept?" Crispus asked him.

"Most of the day, sir. It is now late afternoon. The domina said you were tired and should not be disturbed until cena. I brought a light meal to hold your hunger until then."

"How gracious of her! Please let her know how much we appreciate her kindness." Julia said politely though she was keenly embarrassed to be caught in bed with Crispus.

Petronius nodded. He headed to the door, begging their apologies, and bowing so deep that his nose threatened to hit his knees.

Crispus stretched lazily, then got up to examine the platter of food Petronius left behind. He brought it back to the bed with him. Grabbing a piece of honey honey-drizzled baked apple, he exclaimed "Delicious!" The honey glaze smeared across his mouth and fingers.

Julia laughed at the sight of him. She tossed him a damp cloth Petronius had the forethought to include. "Fine state for a nobleman," she said to him.

Crispus laughed with her, taking the towel. "Noble yes, but a hungry man first." He took another bite before bothering to clean the mess from his face and even then was quick to get back to his food.

Julia had not realized until then how much she missed a good meal amid cozy accommodations. Yet, here Petronius had placed before them a wonderful array of local foods, spiced wine, plump marinated olives, thick cuts of roasted lamb and pungent cheeses. Julia delighted in everything. She took time to savor each bite while Crispus did the opposite. He devoured everything within reach of his hand and drank most of the wine before she could taste a drop.

"You'll suffer for it tomorrow if you don't slow down," Julia chided.

Crispus looked over at her. His eyes were clear despite the wine, but it loosened his tongue. "It would take more than a few cups of wine to rob me of my senses. A fact my stepmother knows well."

Julia looked surprised it him. She had never

heard the full truth of what happened in Mediolanum. Now with wine, food, and a warm bed to lie in, he might be more amicable to talking. "Crispus, what happened that night between you and Fausta?"

There was a stony silence. Julia was about to apologize for asking when the door burst open. Crispus nearly dropped a bite of cheese from his mouth. Both of them turned to see the new intruder.

Licinius' head appeared in the doorway, spilling light from the hallway behind him. He adjusted his eyes to the dim light then spied the scene before him. A bemused grin spread across his face; he opened his mouth to speak, but thought better of it. He eased the door closed with a chuckle.

Neither Julia or Crispus knew what to say. The assumption was mortifying for both of them. Crispus slid to the end of the bed without meeting Julia's eye. Then he walked across the room and with a grunt pushed the giant latch into place. "Licinius thinks the worst, no doubt. At least he won't do it again."

"He knows us better than that – he's just joking. He'll be back in a few minutes," Julia said, dismissing the notion.

"I doubt that. But it's not important in any case. You asked me a question. If you still want to know what happened, I'll tell you. You have come this far with me; you deserve to know everything." Crispus sat down close enough to smell the scent of her hair. Even as it was now, unwashed and tousled, he found it intoxicating. He struggled to keep his focus.

Around them, the fading light of day had capitulated to the dark. Flickering light from the oil lamps bathed the room in ever deepening shadows. Julia gave an involuntary shiver.

"Are you cold? I can have Petronius come back to light the fire." He rose to go, but Julia touched his arm, stopping him.

"No, don't bother. You remember how to start a fire don't you? We don't need to call him."

Crispus was happy for the challenge, "I'm a man of many talents. If you are fortunate, I'll show you some of the better ones."

"And those would be?" Julia said, playing along with his banter.

Crispus pretended to consider the matter as he ignited the fire. He lowered the lamp's flame to the wood. The fire swelled into life with a flash.

"There's wrestling, hunting, fighting and lovemaking, but those two are quite similar actually…and the list goes on." He poked at the fire a few times then came to her side.

"Why does that make you curl up your little nose like that? Don't you know it will get stuck that way?" He tweaked it, making her giggle despite herself. "You ask questions you do not really want answered. Are you sure you want to know what happened with Fausta?

"Well, I don't know. You apparently want me to hear it. I think I know the truth because I know you. Fausta probably tricked you, I've no doubt about that. I do wonder if you truly refused her though. That's the deeper mystery. A ripe body and a lustful man never mix."

At the outrage on Crispus' face she added. "I'm not judging you and I don't fault you for being a man. I don't know that it even matters, really. If you tell me you did exactly what she accuses, what should I do about it? Curse your name, tuck my tail and return home, crying that you deceived me? No, it does not matter to me what happened in Mediolanum. Its enough to know that something did and you are here. I am too. For Helena...and for you," she finished.

"For me? After what happened between us the last time we saw each other? I thought you would hate me forever."

Julia slid away from him. She shook her head a bit to clear it. It was as though just being near him was making it hard for her to think. "I could never hate you, but I did try. I just couldn't manage it—probably never will." Her voice sounded small and weak, even to her. She cleared it, made it stronger. "Not that you didn't deserve it." The hard note of indictment in her tone pleased her, though he bristled at her words.

"Did I? You knew I was leaving to join my father's army, to fight against your father and his allies, no less. What choice did I have? Our families were at war with each other. I was harsh with you because I had to be. Can you not see that?"

"I saw nothing except your back as you ran to tell everyone at the party that you laughed in my face. Why didn't you just run me through with your sword and be done with it? That would have been a kindness."

Patiently, Crispus tried again. "Julia, please listen to me. It had to be done. There were larger concerns than just your hurt feelings. Politics, family loyalty, not being ready for a wife. I had to consider all of it. Although you may not believe it, I acted in your best interest, not just mine. Free of our betrothal, every man of any means at all wanted your hand in marriage. You had your pick. I thought your prospects were better than I could ever do for you, always away at war, always risking permanent damage or worst death."

"Stepping from your door in the morning can get you killed, and what of it that there were other suitors? I wasn't betrothed to them. I didn't want them. I wanted you and I thought you wanted me too. How wrong I was about that! It's not the point now though, and I don't need a lecture. I understand how our world works, even if I don't agree with it. I do not however, understand you. You were cruel when you had no call to be. Why hurt someone you care about if you don't have to?" She was genuinely confused. As she spoke, she hopped from the bed to face him. Her chest rose and fell heavily as she stared him down. Her anger at him came back in a spark of humiliated bitterness that refused to stay inside her. Before she knew what she was doing, she was spewing venom without mercy.

"You are a cold, ambitious, lecherous beast best suited to a brothel than a battlefield. Much more so than the good men you scorn, like my father and grandfather who unlike *your* father don't have any accidental children. You care about nothing except gaining power and position. Your only concern in any of this is your wounded pride. All because your father chose his beloved wife over you, the inconvenient bastard son who betrayed him? As if that was a choice for him to make! Of course he chose a noble wife and their children over the likes of you!"

Crispus was incredulous, the shock on his face

at being spoken to that way was almost comical but he killed her mirth while it was still in her throat with his very poor reaction.

Crispus grabbed Julia and held her tight by her arms. He squeezed her, forcing her to look at him. There was in instant of real danger as his training and his frustration took over and Julia's eyes widened in painful surprise. Ashamed, Crispus released her. He stared down at his hands in disbelief of what they had nearly done.

"Julia, forgive me. I'm so sorry. I don't know what came over me! I would never hurt you! I don't know why I do these things…" he said full of misery and self-loathing.

Julia backed away from him, not sure how to respond.

He moved toward her; his hands raised in surrender. "There is no excuse for mishandling you. I have been in the army too long and grown too casual with violence."

Julia remained unconvinced, she glowered at him until she finally gave in, the battle lost before it began. She dropped her shoulders and plopped down onto the chair in the corner, still far from him. "I'm sorry too. I should not have talked about your father that way but I don't have a brick heart, something you have forgotten more than one. It bleeds and so do I…or I once did, a long time ago." She folded her legs and wrapped her arms around them, once again the young, heartsick girl he disgraced so long ago.

"You and I have hurt each other many times over the years. Perhaps it is time we stopped." Crispus spoke low, his words slightly slurred from the wine.

Crispus came to her then, swaying a bit he knelt down, bringing himself level with her. His face revealed the wine's effect on him. Julia was neither drunk herself, nor unaware that Crispus was not himself. In the heartbeat of time that stretched between them when neither trusted to speak, Crispus decided on a reckless action. Before he could talk himself out of it, he laid his hand gently on her naked thigh where it peeked from beneath her tunic. Neither Crispus nor Julia could breathe as he ran his hands along the length of her leg. Julia trembled again, not from cold this time.

"You shouldn't touch me that way. You're drunk," she whispered but her heart was not in it. "You're not thinking clearly, and neither am I. We should stop this now."

Yet, she made no move to stop his hands from roaming further down her legs. When they reached her feet, he paused to cup them and not even the fire could complete with the heat in his touch. Her feet appeared delicate and tiny under his large, rough hands. He massaged her feet and her calves softly, enjoying the feel of her skin, as it was the finest silk. Julia closed her eyes, suddenly shy and afraid to meet his gaze.

"Why do you ask me to stop? I don't think you really me to do that." Julia opened her eyes.

"How many times have you done this and to how many other girls?"

There was no doubt who was in either of their minds; Cassia with her arms around him, kissing him before the whole city. Julia's heaved and her shoulders shook briefly as the few bites she had eaten threatened to leave her.

"I could give you many reasons why, but the most important is so that we have no misunderstanding between us," she said. In a single movement, she brushed aside Crispus' hands and stood up. She was more confident out of the reach of his inquisitive hands.

She walked away from him then, knowing he would follow her. Julia went to the door where she laid her hand on the latch but did not leave. Instead she turned to him. "Do not mistake me for a plaything to amuse you during the night. I am no merchant's daughter."

Crispus was undaunted by the jab, he came up close behind her. With a gentle hand, missing just a few moments before, he brushed her hair aside to touch his lips to the back of her neck. Something akin to lightning radiated from where his lips lay against her skin, down her spine and lower to places she had only imagined him touching before now. His breath was warm and fruit-scented on her neck. Her knees nearly buckled under the unfamiliar sensation and she grabbed the doorframe to steady herself.

"Julia..." It was just her name but spoken as no one else had ever done before. The sound of it on his tongue right then when he so clearly wanted her, was a promise of something forbidden.

"You say my name as if you mean it, but I have good reason to doubt you, as you well know."

Crispus sighed, summoning patience. "You are not a girl anymore. How long do you intend to punish me for what happened in the past? Yes, you said you loved me, wanted me to stay with you. But we both knew that wasn't possible."

"You're wrong! We might have united our

families and stopped a war. But that's not what your father wanted – nor you. You're just like him, so ambitious and so ruthless. It was more important for you to make your name famous. And so you spurned me, like a slut in the streets. Are you are surprised now that I don't rush into your arms? And if I was so foolish, am I not likely to catch the scent of another on you? You chase women as doggedly as you chase victory and slaughter. Neither are traits I want in a lover, if that's where you imagine this farce is leading!"

She whirled around to face him then and the anger in her eyes made him step back from her.

"You mistake my intentions. You are more than a convenient body for me. I know you're angry, but try to understand me," he pleaded.

"What I see is a man who now values something he tossed aside, and you would have me believe you have experienced an instant change of heart?"

Crispus took her into his arms then. "I don't know what I feel, and that's the truth! I'm as confused as you are, but I am tired of running from everything! This one thing I will face head on!" The strength of his words astonished them both. His arms tightening around her ever so slightly. She tried to resist, but she felt herself weakening as his resolve grew stronger.

Before Julia could react, or he could reconsider, Crispus planted his lips onto hers. His kiss was firm at first then gentler as he felt her respond. With practiced skill, he pushed her lips apart, slipping his tongue in between them. Her arms went around his neck, almost of their own accord. Julia closed her eyes and let herself drown in his kiss, and his enticing, masculine scent.

Crispus pulled her closer still, burying her within the circle of his arms while his tongue danced over hers and circled the inside of her mouth. A cornucopia of rapturous emotions tumbled over them like cleansing rains.

He explored, teased and pushed further, skillfully testing her limits. His hands moved lower. The fire that raced from where their lips touched, traveled with a speed through both of them. Crispus swept a hand under her tunic and there it ended. Julia broke off their kiss, biting his lip in the process.

"Why this violence?" Crispus asked, bewildered. He touched his lip where she bit him and tasted a hint of blood.

"The dog asks the captured bird that pecks him why she does it? Why would I not? I didn't give you permission to lay hands on me the first time either." In a flash, Julia fled his side. She hurried to the bed. Sliding back against the wall, she placed the expanse of the mattress as a barrier between them.

"I would be kissed by a man who means it. And as yet, despite my reaction – you do not. If there comes a time when I believe otherwise, perhaps we will revisit the subject. Until then, do not touch me again without a proper invitation."

Crispus smiled at her naiveté. "As you say, I will not please you again without you asking me for it."

"Please me? You presume too much. Your kiss was nothing to me."

"That's what your mouth says; your body was of a different opinion."

Julia was caught as the evidence of rosy

blossoms spread across her cheeks and to her mouth. Her lips stretched into a smirk she could not stop. She turned away from Crispus and with as much dignity as she could muster, crawled across the bed, and moved around him to unlatched the door. She stormed across the hall to pound on Licinius' closed door.

When he did not answer, she spoke through it. "You can't even face me – you set this up, didn't you? It will not work! I want my room back, and you control your cousin, or I shall do it for you! Now if you two do not mind, I want a bath before we spend the evening with our hosts."

With that, she strode away down the hall; a small slave girl stationed in the hallway struggled to keep up with her and show her the way.

Licinius peeked out from his door. He looked down the hall at Julia's fleeting back then across at Crispus, who stood in the doorway shaking his head. Licinius tried in vain to hold back his laughter. "That went well."

"Better than expected at least." Crispus admitted, before closing the door on a still gleeful Licinius.

Chapter Thirteen

Chance Meetings and Wild Escapades

Cena was an awkward affair that night. Crispus had every intention of showing Basil and his family the greatest of courtesy, but the tension between him and Julia was a distraction for him. He was rude to his hosts without meaning to offend. More than once he heard Emmelia gasp at some word or phrase he used without care, and he found himself repeatedly apologizing for not listening when they spoke to him. *It makes no sense,* he thought. *Why can't I get this nonsense out of my mind? It's never going to happen. She won't allow it.* He slipped a glance at Julia , relieved to find her playing with her food and staring into space lost in her thoughts though she at least answered when Basil or Emmelia spoke directly to her.

The situation was not lost on their hosts. Basil asked pointed questions about their day, including how they found their separate accommodations which he emphasized with marked displeasure. Crispus and Julia knew better than to enlighten him on the sleeping arrangements, they both professed restful sleep and Licinius chimed in to add weight to the claims. Basil was satisfied with their answers and did not press further for which Crispus, Julia and

Licinius who lied on their behalf were grateful.

Reclining on his favorite couch, Basil was in a talkative mood. "My father, may God rest his soul – brought us to these lands twenty years ago. When we arrived, there was already a thriving community here; Christians, runaway slaves and others who needed to disappear. Many other families have been here for centuries, but ours has found its place among the leaders."

Emmelia spoke up then. "I had no idea what to expect from Cappadocia. But we have fared well and suffered no lack of food, money or anything else since we came here. While the agora is not impressive by anyone standards, it is fairly well-stocked, and much of what the rest of the world enjoys can be had here in the wilds if your purse is large enough."

Crispus seized on her words, glad to have some practical and immediate reason for evicting Julia and their kiss from his mind. "That's happy news! My friends and I could use the entertainment of a day at the market, and we have practical concerns as well. The sum to fully replenish our supplies will be high, and if your family has any contacts that could see us to good pricing, I would be grateful." It was as close to asking for charity as Crispus could bring himself. Thankfully, Basil did not need much prodding.

"Of course. Let us take care of it for you. Consider it my gift in honor of Lactantius. I would come with you myself, but my presence will draw unwanted attention to you. Unfortunately, the agora also supplies the garrison at Melitene, which is a half-day's journey from here. Emmelia will escort you in my place and make any purchases you need."

"We will never forget your kindness. One day

soon I hope to return your generosity in double measures."

Emmelia turned to Julia. "A proper trip to market is just the thing for you. You will feel better, my dear, and this long face you are carrying tonight will leave you." She leaned over to pat Julia's cheek. As she did it, her eyes lingered on Crispus, who could not meet her gaze. He turned instead to Julia, who blushed red in response. Emmelia saw all of it. The mystery of their bad manners was solved when Emmelia saw unspoken communication that passed between them. She turned to Basil, who still wore a look of consternation across his face.

She whispered in his ear so that none but he could hear her. "Do not look so fretful about our guests, husband. They are but overgrown adolescents engaged in a game of love. One of them has overplayed their hand, and this strange meal is the result."

"The runaway offspring of rival emperors under our roof ...and we must also deal with teenaged bravado as well. Truly God tests my faith," he fussed. But after that, cena was easier at least for Basil and his wife. They paid Crispus and Julia no mind and spent happy minutes laughing and joking with Licinius, who was more than enough entertainment alone.

After cena, the three friends headed back to their rooms. Julia stopped at the door to the one Licinius had occupied.

"I am taking this room, and we will pretend today did not happen. I don't want to fight with my closest friends. All we have are each other." She looked at both of them. Licinius said nothing; he did not need to do so, they all knew who she was really talking to and why.

Crispus came close to her, backing her against the doorframe. "Of course Julia. I want you to know, I'm full of remorse. I will never step over the line with you again – not until you say so." He kissed her forehead and smiled down at her.

It was a tender moment which Licinius was quick to disrupt. "Well, that's settled then. You two will keep playing your little games, and I will keep laughing at you!" With that he disappeared inside his room. "Come on Crispus – the girl claims she doesn't want you!"

Crispus and Julia just stared after him for a moment in shared amusement at his antics before going into their separate rooms.

As promised, the following morning, Emmelia met them in her vestibule to escort them to the agora. She noticed the change in them immediately. Whatever disagreements had occurred the night before, they were forgotten in the morning light.

"Whatever the disagreement between you, I see you have rectified it," she said to Crispus and Julia.

Crispus spoke for both of them. "Long days on the road wore down our nerves. We hope you will forgive us."

Licinius refused to let that stand. "Speak for yourselves – I was a joy. Isn't that right, Lady Emmelia? It was you two who caused the problem." If he sensed how much his remarks annoyed his friends he didn't show it. He offered his arm to Emmelia.

Emmelia accepted it with grace. "It was our duty and my pleasure. Shall we go?" she said allowing Licinius to lead her from her home. Petronius followed on her heels, along the way giving another servant instruction for the household staff since they would be away for most of the day.

The agora was exactly as Basil described it. There were delights from far flung places but also the conspicuous presence of armed Roman soldiers. The group stopped on the outskirts of it to get an idea of what they would be facing once they went inside the market.

Crispus pulled the hood of his cloak closer about his head. "If our needs were not so dire, I would not frequent this palce. Licinius, Donatus, Quintus, keep your weapons close by. I don't rule out that we may be forced to fight our way out of here. Donatus, I hope you're up for this."

Donatus patted his thigh over the bandages wrapping it. He favored the leg when he walked but he was able to do so unaided. "Of course I am – no scratch on my thigh is going to keep me from my oath. I'm with you as always."

With Emmelia in the lead and Petronius as her ever-present shadow, the group walked through the crowded stalls of the agora. Merchants hawked their wares in loud voices. There were meats and fine wines from the West and of course, the kind of traveling staples Crispus and his companions sought out – wheat, dried meats, nuts and fruits, and horse feed. Quick deals were struck with Emmelia doing much of the bargaining. She was a surprisingly shrewd businesswoman despite her mild manner. While Crispus and the others remained with her during her negotiations, Licinius wandered away to another part of the market for a closer look at a display of fine daggers and swords.

As he moved around some buyers to get a closer view of an array of blades glittering in the sunlight, a girl of similar age to him stumbled into him, striking his chest. Licinius opened his mouth to curse but stopped short. She was near tears and trembling.

"Oh come now. You're unharmed. Don't cry about it!" he told her.

The girl was looking over her shoulder. At the sound of his voice, she jumped in fright. She turned to him. Even with the fear that distorted her features and the tears in her eyes, she was a beautiful girl. Delicate as blown glass, with black hair and violet eyes, she looked to break into a thousand pieces at a touch. Licinius looked behind her to seek out the cause of her distress. He found it right away. An oversized and crazed man barreled towards them with clubs gripped in each hand and murder in his eye. Licinius pulled his gladius from its sheath and braced to defend the girl and himself from the man.

The burly stranger closed the distance between them. He looked past Licinius to the girl cowering behind him. "I will teach you to run from me, you little wench. Your brother cannot save you this time!" the man shouted as he swung the club in her direction.

Licinius shoved the man backwards hard

enough to topple him to the ground. "Stay there if you value your life! You will not lay a hand on this girl!" He laid his sword against the man's exposed throat to drive home his point.

Hearing the commotion, Crispus, Julia and the others appeared at his side in an instant. The young girl cowered behind Licinius. "I'm not his, I'm freeborn! Please make him leave me alone," she moaned with twin rivers of tears flowing down her cheeks.

Julia stepped forward to comfort the girl, placing her arms around her. "Dry your tears. You're safe with us." She pulled her behind Donatus where they would be safest while Licinius, Crispus and the other men dealt with her attacker. "What is your name?"

The girl cast her eyes downward to her presumed captor. His look warned her to silence which only served to loosened her tongue. "My name is Ione and this dog is Pollux. He pretended to be a friend to my father and promised to protect my brother and me while he was away. My father never returned, and Pollux says we're his slaves now. He set upon me this morning, to take from me what I refused to give him, when my brother left for the agora. I saw my chance to escape. I broke a jar of olive oil over his head and ran. He chased me here."

Julia gathered Ione close while Crispus stepped between Licinius and Pollux, who was still lying in the dirt. Licinius pushed him aside; Crispus let it happen curious to see what Licinius had in mind for him.

Licinius leaned over Pollux. In the place of his blade, he put a foot on his neck. He spoke to him with a menacing growl. "You assault this girl without cause? Explain why I should not split your head open for you?"

The villain under his foot struggled to breathe against the pressure on his windpipe. "She lies! Please, let me get to my feet. I can explain," the man pleaded. Before he could say more, another young man, probably the before-mentioned brother considering his haste, pushed his way through the gathering crowd.

The youth rushed to gather the girl into his own arms, then planted desperate kisses all over her face. He had the same raven locks as his sister, but his were curly and cut short. He was clean shaven, dressed in the simple tunic of a peasant, but it was clean and well made. When he spoke, his words were choked with emotion. "Ione, my flower, are you hurt? The neighbors found me. They told me you were running down the street screaming. I feared the worst!"

"Thank God you've come for me! As soon as you left this morning, he tried to force himself on me. I hit him and ran here to find you. This kind man saved me from him," she said, pointing at Licinius, who still had his foot on Pollux's throat. Licinius nodded in greeting.

"I'm Licinius and these are my friends." While he spoke, he ground his foot into Pollux's flesh, eliciting a comical whimper from the man. Licinius leaned down again. "Not so tough now, are you friend? A grown man is a bit different from a frightened girl!"

The newly arrived boy answered for him. "It's a lesson he needed, thank you friend. He would not have dared to do this in my presence. My name is Zosimus. You have met my sister Ione and this viper here in the dirt, is Pollux." Zosimus extended a hand to Licinius who leaned forward to take it. "My gratitude, Licinius. Please move your foot from his throat for just a moment. I want to talk to him."

Zosimus pulled a deadly looking dagger from a leather sheath at his waist and threatened Pollux where he lay. "What did you do to her, dog? I promised you death if you ever touched her, or did you forget?" Before Pollux could voice a lie, Ione quietly whispered her shame into her brother's ear. Fresh tears began to run down her cheeks. On seeing them, Pollux got to his feet while Zosimus was distracted with soothing her. He slid towards the edge of the crowd but didn't get far, before Zosimus was on him.

Before the startled eyes of everyone present, he snatched Pollux's head back, sliced his throat from ear to ear, and let the body drop to gush blood into the streets. The crowd gave a collective gasp but everyone was too shocked to do anything more than gape at the gory sight. No one tried to stop him as he grabbed Ione by the hand and disappeared around a corner. In the confusion that followed, the crowd broke apart and people darted inside their homes and businesses. There would be trouble with the Roman authorities soon and nobody wanted to be around for it. The Romans were notoriously fickle about who else they abused when they came to take a wrongdoer away.

As if under a spell, Licinius followed close on Ione and Zosimus' heels. Before Crispus could stop him or failing that follow as well, he felt a hand on his arm. Looking down, he saw Emmelia who had been silent until now staring up at him, panicked. "You must listen to me, Crispus! Let those people go their way! We must get you out of here before the soldiers recognize you. See there!" She pointed to a structure in the near distance; red-cloaked soldiers poured from it, heading towards the agora.

Crispus knew she was right. "Off the streets and behind me!" he called out to his friends. Julia, Donatus, Quintus and Licinius all rushed to his side. He paused long enough to kiss Emmelia's cheek in gratitude.

"I'm sorry there's no time for a proper goodbye to Basil and you."

Emmelia nodded. "He will understand, just as I do. Now please, go before more soldiers arrive! My slaves and I will do what we can to distract them. All the supplies you need will be waiting for you outside the city by nightfall."

Emmelia put on a fine performance for the crowd, as though she had been an actress all her life. She clutched her stola around her, pulling at it as though it burned her skin. She screamed and fell to the ground near an overturned cart. Petronius dropped to her side, calling for water and aid for the wife of Basil.

While Emmelia and Petronius staged their distraction, the others followed Licinius' pursuit of Ione and her brother to a small dwelling on the edge of the settlement, far from the market. The pair did not lose them among the rock houses of Cappadocia, but rather seemed to pace themselves so the group could follow them. Licinius slowed to allow his friends to catch up to him without losing sight of

Ione. Together approached Ione and Zosimus who were standing on the small doorstep under a sagging cloth awning. The pair went inside, leaving the door slightly ajar behind them.

The group hesitated before going inside. Licinius spoke first, to end the debate before it could start. "I know it looks suspicious, but we have come this far. I think we should go inside. I want to know why they drew us to this place when they could have lost us among the crowds."

Crispus threw up his hands at his cousin. "What is this 'we'? You followed the girl and we followed you rather than lose you!" Crispus emphasized. "I hope this girl is worth the danger. You go first." He pushed Licinius towards the opened door.

Julia encouraged Licinius, when he still hesitated. "Do go on, Licinius! If there are any among us capable of enticing a frightened girl into giving up her secrets, it's you."

Licinius reacted with scorn at her taunt. "The only girls that interest me are those who want to be 'enticed.' I never force, as you well know," he informed her cryptically before he stepped across the threshold into the darkness beyond. For unknown reasons, Julia blushed as she followed in his wake along with the rest of their group.

Once inside the tiny building, they all had to wait for their eyes to adjust to the semi-darkness. Whereas the sun shone brightly outside, just a few of its rays pierced the gloomy interior. Along the darkened walls stood shelves lined with amphorae of all shapes and sizes. Along the floors were sacks marked in Greek labeling the saffron, willow, arsenic, lavender and rose powders, and hemp they held. Running the length of the room was a large wooden counter filled with scales, mixing spoons and other apparatus of the spice business. Ione and her brother stood in front of the counters, waiting for them with eager faces.

"What is this place?" Crispus asked.

Zosimus explained. "This is our father's shop. Pollux was supposed to help watch things but he took it over and forced us to work for him. There was nothing we could do save run away and try to cross the wild lands. That's much too dangerous for us alone, but if you're leaving and allow us to go with you, we'll proof our worth. We have coins and supplies to aid the journey."

"Who says we're crossing the wild lands? We're visiting relatives for a few months, then we're going west, back home to Mediolanum."

We have heard the whispers about the soldiers seeking a great one who is hiding in the city. Your bearing betrays you. You're not simple plebs – we know they're looking for you. And now they will be hunting for all of us, searching door to door until they find us. We cannot stay here. Let us go with you, please. They will be on all of us within the hour!"

While Zosimus was speaking, Donatus had been checking out their surroundings. He pulled up a corner of the heavy canvas covering the windows.

"No, much sooner than that," he said.

Crispus rushed to the door. He opened it just far enough to see what Donatus meant, four soldiers were on their street, combing the area near the shop.

Crispus turned to Zosimus. "Where does the back entrance lead?"

"–To the stables; but there is another way out, a secret way." Zosimus pushed bottles off a shelf unto the floor. He reached for a wooden box set into the wall behind it. Licinius helped him pull the box from its niche in the wall. It acted as a lever to lift the entire wall. Behind it, a small tunnel opened to them. Zosimus grasped the box to smash it against the stone floor. A large canvas bag fell from it along with a few errant gold and silver coins.

Zosimus grabbed the bag, which was heavy from the weight of the treasure inside. "This is our inheritance. We kept it hidden from Pollux." He tossed the bag at Crispus, who barely managed to catch it. He opened it to see the cache of coins. His father's image was reflected back to him hundreds of times in luminous gold.

Zosimus broke his reverie. "Is it enough? Will you take us with you?"

Crispus stared at him, deciding what to do. He thought about Pollux lying dead in the street and knew Ione and her brother would be crucified if they stayed. "Keep your coins for your new life. We only have need of the supplies. You and your sister are welcome to join us if you can help get us to the city gates unseen."

"This tunnel links to an underground passage. It will take us to the edge of the city. From there we can head whichever way suits you."

"Lead the way," Crispus said, and they were off.

As they moved along the pitch-black, narrow passageway, Licinius found a reason and time for jokes. "Pity we cannot take a few of these amphorae with us. Escaping from death traps is thirsty work. A good mulsum is always welcome!" No one laughed, and as always Licinius did not care as long as he amused himself, which he always did.

Chapter Fourteen

Bad Ideas Lead to Bad Ends

The tunnel was a saving grace for Crispus, Licinius, Donatus, Julia and their new friends Zosimus and Ione. When they emerged hours later, their happiness was compounded by the fresh horses and supplies including a heavy purse, they found waiting for them exactly where Emmelia said they would find them.

The thrill of Ione's rescue from Pollux and the dash through the underground passageways bonded the newly enlarged group. The women were especially friendly to each other. Their whispered giggles reminded Crispus that Julia still had much of the young girl he remembered within her.

If it was possible, Julia grew more beautiful during their days on the road. There was something unchained about her, a wildness that reminded him of fires under midnight skies and songbirds free of their cages. Where there had been curves and softness, there were now sharp angles that were far more interesting. She blossomed under harsh conditions that would have weakened lesser women. Crispus could not help noticing the change in her and he wondered if he was the only one to see it.

Traveling with one beautiful woman was

burden enough, but now the men found themselves with two of them, and in hostile territory. By unspoken agreement, the men formed a moving perimeter around them as they passed over the fertile landscape on the way to Karin, where they would find food and shelter before making their final strike towards Yerevan in Armenia.

Ione continued to prove a worthy addition. She was proficient with medicinal herbs and had great skill as a healer. Licinius and the rest of the group found that out in a most unfortunate way. It happened by accident while they were still in the wilderness.

Licinius stumbled upon a scorpion and her nestlings one early morning as he broke down his tent. His shrill screams split the air in the dawn twilight. Everyone dropped their work in alarm and looked for their weapons, sure they were under attack. Donatus rushed to the edge of their campsite ready to defend it. Holding his blades he spun around, frantically seeking an enemy.

Crispus sprung towards his cousin, dagger in hand, though he quickly realized it was of little use with a villain that crawled rather than walked. Instead, he stripped off his cloak to beat at the snapping creatures that surrounded Licinius, attacking him repeatedly.

Crispus managed to avoid being stung himself as he flailed at them with his cloak and stamped out the few that managed to reach him. Beside him, Licinius was beginning to falter from the bites. Ione rushed to him, catching him as he collapsed to the ground. His was sweating, his skin was clammy to the touch, and his breathing fast and shallow, as though it might cease at any time.

As Ione knelt behind him, supporting his head, she wiped away a line of drool that bubbled down his chin. She tried to hold him stationary as his muscles involuntarily twitched. She sent Julia to fetch water for him, but Licinius' shaking was so severe he could not swallow it. The situation was dire and they all knew it.

Ione sent Julia off again, this time to find the supplies she needed. "Quickly! There is a small green vial in my traveling sack. Bring it to me!"

Julia scurried off in search of the antidote. The shaking became violent convulsions that seized Licinius' body beyond Ione's ability to control. Crispus came to her aid, falling across his cousin and pinning him down lest he hurt himself and Ione. Licinius' entire body bucked under the weight, his arms and legs thrashing in every direction.

"Calm, cousin! I have you! I have you!" Crispus shouted. Licinius' frantic thrusts slowed, and then stopped altogether as his breathing became more shallow, and he struggled to fill his lungs. Ione pushed Crispus away and again held him in her arms.

"What is happening? Please, I can't breathe!" Licinius moaned. His eyes rolled into the back of his head. He began to lost consciousness.

Crispus stared down at him, unable to believe Licinius was dying in front of him. "Not this day! You will not die here in the dirt, cousin. Fight!"

Licinius stirred at the words. He struggled to keep his eyes open. Almost too late, Julia appeared back at their side, holding the precious vial that could save him. Ione grabbed it from her, tipped it into Licinius' open mouth then held his lips closed to force the concoction down his throat.

"It burns!" he croaked, clutching at his throat.

Ione was running her hands over Licinius arms and she pointed Crispus toward his legs. "No bites here, how many do you count?"

Crispus stood over him. He counted the tiny punctures still red and bleeding. "He has five that I can see." he told Ione in quiet alarm and dread.

Ione answered him with loud relief instead. "Thank God! He will live! Five stings will sicken him near death, but should not kill him as strong as he is," She cradled his head and Licinius looked up at her, grateful. She pushed his hair aside and kissed his forehead.

"When can we move him?" Crispus asked now that the immediate danger was over. "We should not stay here."

"We can move him now yes, but we should stop for a day or so in the next town so that he can rest properly."

"We're close to Karin. The town is but a half day's journey from here. He can rest in a comfortable bed and recover." Crispus said.

"A pretty woman to share it with me would help. Are you up for it, my girl?" Licinius said, still able to joke. He snuggled his head a little deeper in her lap and closed his eyes.

Zosimus was not particularly amused even if he was glad Licinius was talking. "If you were not already half dead, I would teach you a lesson you would not soon forget." He said, glowering at the injured man. He helped Crispus and Donatus lift Licinius between them, but from the pained grunting, it was plain Zosimus used less care than he should have for someone so grievously injured.

Obstinate as ever, Licinius whined at his rough treatment. "Careful now, I'm not a sack of wheat! Where is the last of the wine? I deserve it for my suffering."

"When is he ever serious?" Julia asked.

"Never" came the answer from both Licinius and Crispus. While they bantered, the other men rigged a hammock of sorts that would allow them to carry him easier between the horses.

Despite the need to move slower to accommodate Licinius, they managed to reach Karin just before sunset. Entering the city was a familiar adventure to them. Karin was far east of Rome and yet it was a typical Roman town complete with dirty, overcrowded streets, drunken men and eager prostitutes and other actors emerging for the night's work. They leered as the group passed them, and though weakened, Licinius managed to pinch the backsides of a few of the woman, promising to come for them when he was back on his feet. All the activity around them was drawing unnecessary attention. They found a nearby bench where Licinius could rest while they sorted out their plans.

"We need to get off the streets and find a place to lay low," Crispus said as he spotted a nattily dressed passerby. The man wore a bright orange and blue tunic and cloak, gold jewelry dripped from his neck, and he wore earrings and gold bands of varying design on his fat fingers.

Crispus brightened at the sight. He knew exactly who and what the man was. "You there!" Crispus called to him. He muttered to his friends, "Just the sort we're looking for..." The man came closer. He sported a full beard and a heavy belly that stretched the shimmering fabric of his tunic to its limit.

"Where are the clean pleasure houses?" Crispus asked with no preamble. As he expected, the man paused with interest rather than shock at his rudeness. Thinking quickly, Crispus motioned to Julia and Ione, who stood beside him. The man looked confused. Crispus added, "I am to offer these foreign wenches for private bidding."

The stranger focused on the women, appraising them as he would any other wares in the agora.

He nodded with the shrewd eye of a connoisseur who spotting a rare find. "Choice, very choice indeed! You have stumbled upon the right man, my friend! Men of the city call me Lenomico. I heard a fresh shipment of brothel slaves arrived today, but I see the best stock has already been taken."

"It certainly has and they should go to the best brothel in the city."

"Around the corner from here is the House of Tiberius Aeliamanus. This one with the purple eyes will fetch a high sum, but the other has a classy look about her that the nobility will love."

"Many thanks." Crispus gave a respectful nod to Lenomico. He turned away to pull the women along with him. Lenomico smiled appreciatively at Julia and Ione once more before going on his way.

As Crispus expected there was an inn and a tavern besides the brothel where they would be no different from any others seeking to disappear into vice in style. Licinius would have a clean bed and an open window for ventilation. He could rest comfortably while he recuperated from his injuries, and in all went well, no one would give them a second glance for the days they would need to be in the city.

Instead of retiring to their rooms, everyone except Licinius, who they carried up to his bed, sat in the inn among the other guests. Over cups of wine and a hearty meal of roast pork and lentils, Ione and Zosimus provided more details about their early life with their father. They were Greeks, born on the island of Crete. After their father divorced their mother for infidelity, he took them and left Crete. He traveled deep into the empire and settled them in Cappadocia. Now that he was presumed dead they wanted to rejoin their family on Crete and see the mother they had not laid eyes on since they little more than toddlers.

"How do you know she lives?" Julia asked.

Zosimus smiled softly. "My heart would tell me so." His words were filled with despair and longing as only a motherless child can conjure. Beside him, Ione's eyes filled with tears.

Julia took her hand. "May the Christ you believe in guide you home." Ione's eyes widened in shock. "Do not look so surprised, Ione. I know that you're a Christian. You need have no fear of discovery with us. My mother is a Christian and so is Crispus' grandmother."

"But not you?" Ione looked from Julia to Crispus.

Julia touched Crispus' arm, silencing the words she knew would hurt Ione before he spoke them. With care she said, "Not yet, but I am convinced more each day of this journey. I know some divine purpose is guiding us, where it will lead I cannot say."

"I pray that safety follows you, and the peace of Christ finds you." She stood. "I will say goodnight now and goodbye. My brother and I make for Crete in the morning."

Crispus was confused. "Morning – you part ways with us? We thought you planned to travel east with us? We could use Zosimus' help. We have much ground to cover and enemies all around us."

Zosimus spoke for them. "I'm sorry, but it is impossible. Our path leads south. Please understand. We turn southward, to the coast, where we may put our coins towards passage home."

Crispus thought of his own mother, taken from him before he could really come to know her. He tried to conjure her in his mind, but her image was a blurred distortion, distinct only in his memory of the love she bore for him.

"No, I would not delay your return to a mother who yet lives. I would give anything to be able to see mine again," Crispus said with resignation.

"Was she a Christian?" Ione asked him.

"Perhaps; I never had the chance to ask her," Crispus answered.

"Heaven waits for all those who accept Christ. If your mother did, and before you die, you come to know the truth as well, you will see her again, on the other side of heaven."

Crispus did not trust himself to speak. The idea that he might once again see his mother's face gave him a hope he had not experienced in a long time.

"I hope so, Ione," was all he could say to her.

His eyes began to mist. He changed the subject before the mist became tears that would embarrass him. "We should all retire to our rooms. Tomorrow will be a long day for all of us."

Everyone stood to leave. As they did, Julia noticed a familiar face amongst the revelers.

"Is that not the man we spoke to on the edge of town? I wonder if he followed us here."

Crispus studied the man. "No doubt he owns this place too. See how the slaves behave around him. He's their master; I'm sure of it. He bears watching, I agree with you but do not worry. You and Ione will be across from us. We will hear it if a mouse passes by your door."

Julia was skeptical. "I did not care for the way his eyes fell upon us, but as you say." She took Ione by the hand. "Come, if this is to be our last time together; I would spend it without the men spoiling it with their presence."

"Have no fear ladies, we would not think of intruding on your night. We have our own affairs to attend. Come on boys, let's get some wine and keep Licinius company, though he will probably outdrink us as he usually does." With that Crispus and the other men headed to Licinius room, right across the hallway from the women.

"Julia?" Crispus knocked again on the door. The men had been up for at least an hour, despite nursing headaches from enjoying being in a safe, warm place a little too much. Knowing their fondness for each other, they decided to allow Julia and Ione more time to awaken on their own and say their goodbyes, but the morning was slipping away, and still the ladies did not appear.

"It's time to leave!" Crispus knocked harder, but there was still no response. Frustrated, head throbbing and with angry words ready for Julia, he pushed hard against the door. It was unlocked and opened with ease. The room was in disarray with obvious signs of a struggle and the women nowhere to be seen. In an instant his pain fell away under a cloud of trepidation, confusion and guilt. "Zosimus! Come quick! They're gone!" he shouted down the hallway.

Almost before Crispus could finish speaking, Zosimus raced from their room to stand beside him in the open doorway. He looked around frantically. "What are you saying? Where is my sister? Who had the last watch?" He looked to the Crispus, Donatus and Quintus who all just looked around at each other without answers. It was clear there had been no last watch and it was everyone's fault.

Zosimus turned to shout down the stairs behind him. "Ione! Ione! Where are you?" From below them, there was a loud scraping sound then a crash of pottery falling to the floor. Crispus and Zosimus exchanged relieved expressions. They both turned to the stairwell to wait for Julia and Ione to appear.

Instead it was Licinius who emerged into the hallway, wine cup still in hand, some of it staining his tunic. "Damn that maid! When you shouted, she dropped a jar of wine tying to refill my cup. I heard you call Ione's name. Are they ready then? Ione's herbs worked miracles. I'm feeling myself again this morning, thank goodness!"

Zosimus shouted at him. "No, she isn't ready! She is gone, both of them! Look at this room. Something terrible has happened!"

Licinius saw the room but for once he was the voice of calm reason while the other men were near panic. "Perhaps they're in the latrine or went to the agora. I'll take Donatus and check." Licinius disappeared back down the stairs with Donatus in tow.

The latrine was only a short distance away. Licinius returned quickly with the report that they were not there either. The men waited anxiously for Donatus to return from the agora, the last hope of finding them if all was well. When he returned also absent Julia and Ione, all hearts dropped and so did their heads in shame and guilt.

"Ione is all I have left in this world. I know someone has stolen her away! How could we let this happen?" Zosimus was almost hysterical with worry.

Crispus did his best to pull his thoughts together. "They would never leave on their own, yes someone has taken them. Where is that leno from last night?"

"He is still here, the arrogant fool! I just saw him a while ago. If he did not do this thing, he knows who did." Licinius said, racing back downstairs. The other men took off after him. As Licinius went down, he pulled his dagger from its sheath. Crispus and the others unsheathed theirs as well. There was no plan other than to use them, if they could, to carve up whoever had stolen Julia and Ione from them.

When Licinius reached the main room of the

inn, he went straight to the far corner where the man from the night before was sitting with a loaf of bread and an amphora of wine in front of him. Before the man knew what happened, Licinius had snatched him by his garish robes and placed his blade against the man's throat.

"Tell me where our women are if you value your life," he growled. Licinius was fearsome in his anger, a raging, scar-faced bull on the attack. All signs of sickness were gone. The rotund man signaled to his bodyguards who stood across the room but seeing the well-armed, hostile men around him, they did not intervene. They stood whispering together in a fierce debate, proving as always good help is hard to find.

Just to be sure, Crispus flashed his blade at them. Zosimus, Donatus, Quintus and he closed in on the guards. Zosimus told them with true malice, "If any of you interfere, I'll send you to the afterlife right now! Ask yourself if this wretch is worth it." The guards faded back into the crowd of drunken gamblers, and then to the door, evidently deciding he wasn't. The leno pleaded for his life, seeing his people desert him.

"Please, I don't know what you're talking about! Release me!"

"Oh, I will release you – from this world if you do not tell me where they are," Licinius said.

"Who?" he moaned. "Who are you looking for?"

Licinius lost his patience. He sliced the man across the face drawing blood down his cheek. "You know full well we're looking for the women we had with us! Someone snatched them in the night. You have been covering them since we entered this city.

You tell me where they are, or I will carve your heart from your chest! You decide right now if you want to live or die!"

When the man hesitated, Licinius thrust the blade deep into his thigh. The man screamed in agony but he loosened his tongue with no further delay.

"Aghh! I'm sorry. I sold them! Please, I did not know they held so much value to you. Here, I'll split the money with you. Let me get my purse!"

Zosimus stepped forward to cuff the man roughly about the head. "Do you think I would sell my sister to the likes of you? We're going to ask one more time – where are they?" He pointed the tip of his blade at the rouge's eye. "You think I'm playing games with you?"

Crispus stepped forward to place a warning hand on Zosimus' arm. "Let me talk to him."

Both Zosimus and Licinius were too angry to move. "Now." Crispus commanded softly. Zosimus and Licinius reluctantly stepped back.

Crispus spoke quietly to the man. "If you don't want more pain and misery than you have ever had in your life, you will answer us or die right here." For some reason, he believed Crispus' calm promise more than Licinius and Zosimus' loud threats. He spoke up without hesitation.

"Ctesiphon. I sold them to a trader, and he's taking them there to offer them to the Persian elites – please do not kill me. I have told you the truth!"

Licinius' blade dropped from the man's throat. They stood in shocked silence. Of all the places in the world, Julia was on her way to one that would doom her, and Ione with her. Roman women suffered more than others did when Persians captured them. It was an act of vengeance for years of fighting between their nations. Now an imperial daughter headed into the Persian capital. Crispus could only imagine what horrors she would face from the Persian scum who purchased her.

Zosimus, on the other hand, had no idea the danger threating Ione. "Why do you wince that way? What is this place? Tell me!"

Crispus filled him in gently. "It is not the place, but the people. They will tear Julia and Ione to pieces for amusement. Julia's father Galerius Augustus took the Persian King Narseh's family as war spoils and refused to return them. His daughter will be a valuable prize, and with a beautiful handmaid thrown in, the Persians will show no mercy. This dog has sold them into hell! Death would be kinder."

Zosimus shook his head as if to clear it of a horrible, distressing image. "I don't care where they have taken them, I will go into the jaws of hell to find Ione. We must rescue them!"

Crispus and Licinius agreed. Helena would have to wait. He clasped hands with Zosimus. "We will see them safely back to us or die trying."

Licinius agreed. He turned back to the quivering man. "Tell us everything you know!" he demanded again.

The man swallowed hard against the dagger placed back at his throat. He revealed all he knew about the taking of Julia and Ione. When they were sure he had nothing else of value to tell them, Quintus took him behind the inn and cut his throat for him. They needed to get away quickly before his death was widely known and the body discovered. Surely someone would be around to avenge him and they intended to be far away by the that time.

As the fat leno bled out in the dust and grime, Zosimus cried out, "It's a pity we can only kill him once!" He knelt and stabbed the man as many times as he could in a blind rage.

Crispus and Licinius let him do it for a bit then pulled him off the man's body.

"Come away, Zosimus," Crispus said. "There is no time to lose! They are hours ahead of us, and the distance is increasing, the longer we linger here. This scum is not worth another thought. Let us go rescue those we love!" He realized, not for the first time, that he loved Julia and would not rest until she was back in his arms.

Locations in Blood Empire

Cappadocia:

More Thomas. McLean Susan. Arion: A Journal of Humanities and the Classics Third Series, Vol. 19, No. 1

Chisholm, Hugh, ed. (1911) Encyclopedia Britannica (11th ed). Cambridge University Press

Dawkins, R.M. (1916). Modern Greek in Asia Minor. A study of dialect of Silly, Cappadocia and Pharasa. Cambridge University Press

On a Poisonous Cappadocian
(Greek Anthology 11.237)

A viper that bit a Cappadocian died
At once from drinking blood so putrefied.

Cappadocia is a beautiful and ancient land where the hardiest people in the world lived, died and hid from religious persecution. The earliest records of the land date from the 6th century BC when it belonged to Darius I and then his son, Xerxes. Then it was called Katpatuka meaning 'land of the beautiful horses.' The land is hot and dry with cold winters with a unique landscape of rock formations in spectacular shapes and sizes.

The unique terrain made for perfect hiding places for early Christians seeking escape from the merciless persecutions of the Roman emperors. Cappadocia in the home for several underground cities built by Christian refugees, Kaymakli now a major tourist attraction for the region, is one of them. The cities were dug into the soft volcanic rock by the early Phrygians and then reused by the Christians who expanded them to include chapels.

Library of Celsus

Ephesus Ancient City. Selcuk Izmir Turkey. (2004-2015). Celsus Library retrieved from www.ephesus.us/ephesus/celsuslibrary.htm

The Library of Celsus was renowned as one of the most beautiful monuments in a city that held one of the seven wonders of the world at the time, the Artemision. The library was built in 117AD by Gaius Julius Aquila to honor his father, Gaius Julius Celsus Polemaeanus who was a former governor of Asia and an extremely popular Ephesian statesman. Celsus himself is entombed beneath the library which was a rare honor since people were usually not buried within the city limits and certainly not within a library.

The Library of Celsus was ranked third in beauty and renown behind only the Great Library of Alexandria and the Library of Pergamum. It was destroyed more than once by fire and earthquake and was rebuilt. Only the façade remains now, but it reveals the majesty and scope of the building so that one can imagine how it appeared in its glory days.

Nicomedia

Ancient Worlds, LLC. (2002-2013). Nicomedia retrieved from www.ancientworlds.net

Nicomedia came to prominence in the Roman world when Emperor Diocletian makes it his capital when he introduced the tetrarchy. The city was important to Constantine as well. He served in Diocletian's court from Nicomedia in his youth, was educated and died in a villa just outside of it in 337 AD.

Nicomedia remained an important city to the Romans even after the founding of Constantinople (Constantine's treasure city) owing to the fact that several important roads to converged in the city.

The city was nearly destroyed by an earthquake in the mid-fourth century and a fire shortly thereafter nearly finished it. It was rebuilt but never reached its former glory.

Imperial Coinage

Crispus, circa 323 — After the defeat of the Goths

Constantine, circa 313 — To mark his victory in 312

Fausta, circa 323 — After being named Augusta

Excerpt from...*A Day for Tears & Triumph*

The following morning the guards violently shook Julia and Ione awake while the sky was still dark. Cursing at them, the men dumped them unceremoniously into the common room with the other girls. The room blazed with lamp light as though it was full morning instead of the edge of dawn. Titus was there, lounging on his couch. He was awake and already drunk. The room was cloudy with smoke. The pungent odor of burning hemp came from a small bowl a slave girl held at the ready. Every so often, he took great sucking breaths from it, emerging from the smoke red-eyed and smiling. He appraised the confused and still drowsy girls.

"Who will I taste this morning?" Titus pretended to ponder the question, but his gaze never wavered from Ione's face. "I'll have the raven-haired beauty again. I don't want her bathed but as she is. Come here girl," he commanded. He brutally shoved his hand up Ione's tunic. Ione gasped at the pain of his unwanted invasion. Titus closed his eyes. He ran his finger under his nose, grunting in excitement.

"You're as fresh as the morning!" exclaimed. He breathed as deep of her scent as he had his bowl of hemp. "The rest of you...out!"

The other girls were happy to comply. Only Julia lingered a moment. Titus perked up at the sight. "You wish to join us? Perhaps I'll take just a little of you, not enough to spoil my price." Not wanting to see Julia at his mercy with her, Ione moved between them. She offered Titus a smile that anyone except him could see was contrived.

"Please, there is no need... you may do as

you like," she pleaded. Seemingly enticed, he waved Julia toward the door. She followed the others from the room as Ione loosened her tunic from her shoulders and closed her eyes. The last thing Julia saw as she closed the door was Titus' fat, greedy hands snatching at her friend. It was then that Julia shed her first tears in a very long while. As she wiped them away, she wondered how she could trust a god who allowed his faithful daughters to suffer under men like Titus.

For the next several weeks, it was more of the same for Ione. Titus favored her above all others in his house. He called for her nightly, though fortunately for Ione, he was often very drunk and easily pacified. Julia remained untouched as promised but the question of exactly whom they were saving her for lingered. Ione offered prayers daily. In her fledging faith, Julia could not help but notice they went unanswered.

Finally, Lydia broke the news that sealed Julia's fate, for better or worse. She came to them late one morning, after the customers were gone from the house and everything was still. When she stole into their room, Ione and Julia lay huddled together in Julia's bed. Titus has been especially rough with Ione hours before and Julia comforted her. Lydia called their names softly and then she whispered the bad tidings to them.

The personal envoy of King Adhur Harseh of Persia was coming for Julia in a few days' time. Julia did not need to be told anything else about him. The newly crowned King of Persia was known by every Roman. He was famous for his cruelty and his penchant for exotic means of causing suffering and pain. The stories about him were the stuff of legends Julia hoped could not possibly be true. According to Lydia, King Adhur paid well for the privilege of owning Julia. Messenger birds had flown back and forth for weeks until Titus was finally able to settle on a price, richer than he expected.

Julia's mind reeled from the tale when Lydia finally revealed all of it. "A hundred thousand gold darics he paid for you," Lydia stopped to take Julia's hand for the rest of her news in a display of uncharacteristic kindness. "Ione is to remain here." Lydia's face changed at the mention of Ione staying behind. The notion did not please her either.

Ione was aghast. "I won't last in this place with you!" She jumped from the bed to throw herself into Julia's arms.

Julia stroked Ione's hair and whispered comforting words. She looked to Lydia. "I would see us gone from this place before they arrive. Is such a thing possible? Titus will give you nothing for me, but help me and I will see you rewarded beyond your dreams. More than enough for you to buy your freedom and leave this place forever, if you wish it so."

Lydia gave a guarded answer. "It might be possible, if you can tell me why I should trust you to keep your word once you are free of this house."

Julia was ready for her. "–Because you can't afford not to believe me. Do you want to see your status in peril because Ione remains here, in easy reach of Titus, when you could buy your freedom in a matter of weeks? We have dealt fairly with each other so far and Titus is ignorant to our plans. You can trust me." Julia paused and she waited for Lydia. The weight of the world lay in her answer.

"I'll see both of you away from here if I can without risking my life, but if you are caught –"

Julia's heart leaped in her chest. "We won't be," she said, resolutely. She suppressed an urge to celebrate as a sliver of caution interrupted her glee. Lydia's declaration was comforting, but there was no way to be sure she was trustworthy. Julia searched the girl's face for any sign of betrayal just as Lydia had studied hers before saying yes.

"You do this from your heart or your head?" Julia demanded to know.

"Both. I do it because it benefits me. Because I want you both gone. For my own reasons, and since the two of you arrived Titus talks of nothing except Ione's pleasures and the girls he can buy after he sells you. I have a good life here. Hard-earned from years on my knees and I will not lose it now just because a new little tigress has his attention."

Julia was still unmoved. "I ask the same question you asked me. What stops you from betraying us? Why not tattle to the guards? That would accomplish what you want, at no risk to you."

Lydia shook her head in exasperation. "Have it your way then. If you want my help, you have my price." Without another word, she turned and walked away, leaving Julia and Ione alone.

Julia breathed a sigh of relief. She would have her freedom. A plan had been forming in her mind since the morning she watched Ione sacrifice her dignity to Titus to protect her. She confided her true intentions to Ione. She was met with unexpected resistance, particularly when she shared her idea for getting past Titus. Julia had resolved to poison him.

"It will never work! You expect to get close enough to his cup to poison it? And what then? The guards will just allow us to walk away because Lydia says so? You're going to get us both killed!" Ione whispered, angry and scared. They were huddled together on Julia's bed with a blanket shared between them. A cool breeze flowed through the room.

Julia's hands shook, but not from the air. "You can stay here if you like but I am no slave. If I have a chance to run, I'm going to take it! Lydia is offering that chance."

"I want my freedom too, but not at the cost of my life. Titus would not dare kill you, but me – he'll tear into pieces to feed the dogs." Ione said with a certainty Julia could not question.

Julia recalled the sounds that came from Titus' room when Ione was trapped inside. She could only imagine what she endured at his hands so she did not question his cruelty. Julia tried again. "Do you not recall freedom? Would you not risk all to know the sweetness of it again? It is a precious thing, more than life and worth the ultimate sacrifice. Titus is the only thing standing in the way. Should we not remove him any way that we can?"

"With all my heart, I desire freedom. But, I won't have blood spilled on my account. Titus can't die by our hand! No matter what he has done I will not have it on my head. Swear it Julia! You won't kill him."

Julia was dumbfounded. After all Titus had done to Ione this was the last thing she expected. Out of love for Ione she relented, but only a little. "He won't die. The amount will be too small to kill him, only send him into a deep sleep, which is more than he deserves. By the time he comes around, we will be gone from this place."

Julia went on to describe how she intended to sneak mandrake root into Titus' wine. The next time he called for Ione, she would leave the door ajar. While he was well distracted with her, Julia could slip into the room and put the root into his drink. "Easy as a morning rain…"

"But you said yourself it could kill him. What if he has too much and he dies after all?" Ione fretted.

All this for a man they both detested, Julia's goodwill wore thin. "And what of it? Titus is more beast than man. Robbing him of his miserable life is a kindness!" She stopped to lay a gentle hand on Ione's arm. The poor girl's heart was too tender for her own good. "These worries should be far from your mind. If I feel no hesitation or fear, why should you feel any for me? This will see both of us free." They went over the plan several more times, each time ending with Ione in doubt and Julia in frustration.

Finally, Ione offered a concession. "If it must be done. I'll do it myself, so no one else will suffer for it. I'm the one most wounded by him." she added.

Julia was patient. "You have said it before. He never takes his eyes off you. How are you going to manage it? Will you put something into his cup, smile and wait for him to swallow it?" Inspiration took fire in Julia's eyes. "Perhaps that is not such a bad idea. Titus will take anything from your hand. Perhaps he'll take his downfall as well."

It was not possible for her to be pleased at the idea, but Ione was at least satisfied. Truthfully, Julia did not intend to leave her freedom up to the girl but there was no harm in letting Ione think so.